MURDER BY FAX

Books by Elsinck:
  Tenerife!
  Murder by Fax
  Confession of a Hired Killer

MURDER BY FAX

by

ELSINCK

translated from the Dutch by H.G. Smittenaar

NEW AMSTERDAM PUBLISHING, Inc.

ISBN 1 881164 52 7

Printing History:
1st Dutch printing: June, 1991
2nd Dutch printing: December, 1991

1st American edition: 1992

Cover Design: Studio Combo (Netherlands)
Typography by Ten Point Type, Washington, D.C.

MURDER BY FAX

In any murder case, two people always know the perpetrator. However, one doesn't want to talk and the other will never talk again.

****

The game begins!

Day after tomorrow, January 8, 1990, our first fax will be sent to "Target". All details have been prepared. With patience we will reach the goals we have set. The organization we are dealing with, will try anything to localize and eliminate us. We must be prepared for that and we must think and act as they do. As agreed, for the time being, the initiative will be from my side only. Under no circumstances must you contact "Target", regardless of the apparent urgency and necessity of the circumstances. Impulsive actions can wreck the successful completion of our plans. We can depend on our adversaries to try every possible tactic to make us act precipitously. We must be constantly alert against that eventuality. Therefore all communications will be by fax. Between you and me as well as between us and "Target". All faxes sent within our organization must be stripped of any identifying marks. All indications as to origin, day or date must be removed. No names must be mentioned. A received fax must be burned immediately after reading. All information must be memorized, not written down. Sending and receiving of all faxes must be between 19:00 and 19:30 Dutch time. It is important that your fax machine is in a space that cannot be infiltrated by unauthorized personnel on transmission days. Transmission days have been set for alternate even and odd dates for each week, starting with week 3, odd. Although we are certain that fax communications cannot be intercepted and Dutch Law prohibits taps on fax lines, these safety measures must be maintained.

Confirm receipt by return fax.

You know the number that will reach us.

++

Communication received and understood. It has been a long time since
action was decided upon, but we cannot be too careful. A good start for
the New Year. 1990 will be the year of truth and will bring us what we
expect. You can trust me. I have been trained to deal with matters
precisely and thoroughly while anticipating the unexpected. I have used
the past months to make contacts that can be of use to us in the times to
come. There will be no mistakes, everything is now just a matter of time.

Waiting for further instructions.

RADICAL PEOPLE'S FRONT FOR AFRICA

number of pages: 1   to: Mr. Voute, Shell Netherlands

8 January, 1990

!!!! FREEDOM FOR BLACK AFRICA !!!!

The freedom fight of the black peoples of Africa shall be long. The white minority still rules with an iron fist and new president F.W. de Klerk reacts in the same way as his predecessors. The recent measure to open all beaches for blacks does not change that. Supported by multi-national organizations such as Shell and other, imperialistic, Western money hyenas, change or democratic rights for more than ninety percent of the African population is unreachable. We are an organization that wants to help. However, we disassociate ourselves from the acts of vandalism that so recently have plagued Shell. A struggle is necessary; it is inevitable. Therefore we seek support. A time will come when power will shift to the black peoples of Africa. Everyone and every organization who now commits to the struggle for victory, will be received with open arms by the new rulers of a new Africa of the future. Again, we do not want to destroy and we don't want anarchy. We want financial support for the struggle which is inevitable. Victory is a foregone conclusion. There is incontrovertible proof that the will of the majority of more than ninety percent of the African population can no longer be suppressed. Help to shorten the battle, help to save lives and assure yourself a future in the new Africa.

We ask you for a contribution of US $5,000,000.

Place a classified ad in the 'Telegraaf' for Saturday morning, January 13, under the heading 'Greetings and Wishes' with the text:

"Dear RPFA, I want to help. S."

ATTENTION: Mrs. J.A. Sijtsma
            Headquarters Administration

BRUNEI, January 8, 1990

Dear Janny:

First of all a Happy 1990 from all of us. A little late but let's make believe it's because of the distance. Here is hoping that we can remain healthy and eternally young, right?

Well, here I am, in the Shell compound in the middle of the jungle among the Ibo's. The trip was without incidents, hardly any delays and the service was excellent. Our little girl had a slight attack of angina when we left Holland, so it wasn't a lot of fun for the child. But the stewardesses were angels for her. Our own KLM is still my favorite. Arie and Yvonne Staverman picked us up. She said she knew you. They live in Maasland. She is dark blonde with glasses, a little bit of a schoolteacher type, and he is a real sportsman. Darling people, who helped us a lot during the first few days, because you have to get used to it, you know. Boss Shell takes care of his slaves, but you must be able to adapt. The houses are fantastic. Roomy, lots of balconies, all the appliances you might wish. Compared to this, our apartment in Voorburg is no more than a chicken coop. The moment we got off the plane, the heat attacked us like a warm, wet blanket. 42 degrees!!! (Centigrade = 106 Fahrenheit, trans.) I lost it for a while. You may not believe this, but for the last week I have had a cold, in this heat!! But I have already bought some Dutch cough drops in the Shell store. Imagine, cough drops in the jungles of Brunei. It is ridiculous. When you enter the compound store it is like entering a grocery store in Amsterdam. Chocolate bread spreads, Leiden cheese, sweet and sour pickles, all the Dutch foods. And let's not forget pea soup and kale with sausage in tins. Imagine, pea soup and 106 in the shade. They are all really nice here. It is a sort of bungalow park without rent. No matter what you want, they have it. Antje's hair is almost bleached white from the swimming pool. That's where she spends her days. In a few days she'll start Kindergarten but I don't think she wants to go. We went to look and introduce ourselves, but she didn't like it. There are also all kinds of clubs open for membership. Chess, tennis, stage, crafts, you know what I mean. A lot of attention is given to all the Dutch holidays such as St. Nicholas, Christmas (2 days) and the Queen's Birthday. Every excuse is good enough to organize something, even the victory of the 80-year war (with Spain, 1568-1648, trans.). Last Christmas was very nice. A sort of church service in the canteen and then of course, the Christmas story, performed by the little ones. Antje was upset that she could not participate. New Year's Eve was also real cozy. Now everybody is getting ready for Mardi-Gras. I play tennis each morning. Ben and I think we'll be able to survive the next five years. We cannot spend any money here and we don't have to pay taxes, so we'll probably return rich. The second day we bought a jeep from an English family who were being rotated back home. Real macho. We have also been inside the jungle. Exciting.

How are you all? Let us hear something from you. I must say I miss you. It is a nice adventure, but I'll miss going out with you. Will you greet everybody for us?

Love from us all for you two.

Will you write soon?

Carla

Amro Bank

FAXBERICHT/FACSIMILE MESSAGE

NAAM/NAME	T.A.V./ATTN:
Mr. W.W. Stork	XXXXXXXXXXXXXXX

VAN/FROM	
J. van Ginkel	AMRO, THE HAGUE

DATUM/DATE	HANDTEKENING/SIGNATURE
8 January, 1990	

Dear Mr. Stork:

In order to bring you up to date, we want to give you a summary of the options that will be due on January 26, next.

					quotation +/-	
Open/Sell	50 cal	Akzo	JAN 130	141.50 -/- f	57,500.00
" "	30 put	NedLloyd	JAN 100	89.50 -/-	33,000.00
" "	50 put	V.O.C	JAN 40	35.50 -/-	22,500.00
" "	60 put	Wessanen	JAN 90	61.50 -/-	17,100.00
" "	50 put	Ahold	JAN 150	135.00 -/-	75,000.00

Total NEGATIVE (Debit)   f 359,000.00

We request that you arrange for a deposit of f 350,000.00 (three hundred and fifty thousand guilders) to decrease the margins created by above negative results.

Sincerely,

J. van Ginkel

J. van Ginkel (director)

TO MRS. CARLA VINK

9 January, 1990

Dear Carla:

I'll write you right back before I put it off, or I am snagged by one of the bosses. To you all, also, best wishes for 1990. Everything here is "same old, same old". Busy. I miss you already.

I went to your apartment last week and everything is still there. I also took a look at the mail, but I did not see anything that should be forwarded. You did forget to cancel road tax assessment for the car. I have done it and forged your signature. I thought it would be a shame to spend the money with the car in the garage. So, I saved you that, at least. Your neighbors upstairs, are real nice people and they will keep an eye on things for you. I picked up the laundry and put it away in the closet. You see, you are being taken care of, while you loll around in the swimming pool. Frank had a collision with his new car, last Friday. It was his fault. For days he was not fit to live with. Everything is fixed now and he is happy again. Men and cars!

I know Yvonne Staverman really well, will you give her my best wishes? The last I heard was that she was scheduled to return to Holland soon, or has that been cancelled? I thought they have been there for some years, or not? Let me know sometime. Just before Christmas I talked with Mr. Voute about the possibility of part-time work. I told him that we would like to have a child and I cannot combine that with a full-time job. He seemed a bit disappointed. He is a nice man and I have been with him for fifteen years. But, what do you want, I am 38 and if I don't do it now, it's never going to happen and he understood that. We agreed that I would work half days as soon as I got pregnant. I have started to train Annette to take over. Let's hope we'll be successful. So, you'll understand that Frank and I have been going to bed rather early for the last few weeks. Now he can even watch the Playboy Channel, as far as I am concerned. And guess what! I am knitting! If that isn't final proof of developing motherhood, I don't know what is.

Everything is fine with Mother. She is still a bit weak but then, it was a difficult operation. She lives with Ans and is really being spoiled. Every day, after work, I stop by. The divorce of Ans is going to be final. Thank God, everybody is being reasonable, no quarrels and accusations. He has promised her an alimony that is going to be more than sufficient and she keeps the house. Knowing my sister, she'll want to redo the whole thing. The children spend the week-ends with him and it seems to go well. It should always be this way, I think, I always found him to be a good guy and I have not been mistaken. Too bad it didn't work out. He doesn't have anybody else, that's become clear.

Darling, I'll stop. Let me know something about you as soon as possible, tell me everything that's happening because I am dying to know.

Janny

Restaurant
Tristan

Proprietaire: Francois le Roi
Zandpad 24
1439 BK Wassenaar
Telephone: ЖЖ7ЖЖ3ЖЖ8Ж34
Fax: ЖЖ9ЖЖ57Ж3ЖЖ2

To Management Shell Netherlands
ATTN: Mrs. J.A. Sijtsma
Rotterdam

Wassenaar, 9 January, 1990

Dear Mrs. Sijtsma:

In response to your visit and our verbal agreements, I hereby confirm your reservation for approximately 100 persons for a dinner-dance on next March 10 on the occasion of the 25-year anniversary of Mr. Voute.

By separate carrier I will be sending you a contract.

Please be so kind as to sign and return it.

Within the week I will also send you several menu suggestions for selection by Mr. Voute.

As soon as more details regarding the program for the evening have been settled, I hope you will let me know.

With friendly greetings,

15

RADICAL PEOPLE'S FRONT FOR AFRICA

number of pages: 1   to: Mr. Voute, Shell Netherlands

15 January, 1990

!!!! FREEDOM FOR BLACK AFRICA !!!!

We did not find an advertisement in the 'Telegraaf' on Saturday morning
which could have indicated that you want to support our struggle. We will
assume that this is the result of a misunderstanding. We understand that,
during this phase of the negotiations, you will want to know more about
our organization. You must appreciate, however, that we are in no position
to reveal our identity. Traitors never sleep and the spies for F.W. de Klerk
are everywhere. Black Africa needs weapons. People are fighting with
bare hands against a well armed and trained fascist army. Innocents are
killed and buried in mass graves. Prisons are filled with freedom fighters
who want nothing more than democratic rights for everyone. Torture and
intimidation are the order of the day. It is difficult to fight against tanks and
armored vehicles with bare fists. This can become a struggle to last years
whereby many innocent lives will be lost. We want to shorten the struggle.
They need weapons and supplies. We want to help. Therefore we ask for
financial support. Your interests are also at stake. Call it an insurance
premium to protect the continuance of your interests in that part of the
world. $5,000,000 is a small amount for a multi-national like Shell.

Place a classified ad in the 'Telegraaf' for Thursday, January 18, under the
heading 'Greetings and Wishes' with the text:

"Dear RPFA, contact me. S."

****

As predicted, there was no reaction to fax 1 of phase 1. Meanwhile "Target" has received fax 2. Let's wait. Listen around, all information is important. Try to renew contact with old friends. You know who. I don't expect immediate results, but we have time. We must slowly bring this situation to a crisis. It will have to start innocently, like pin pricks. Sooner or later they will answer, we can bank on that. Nobody knows us and the fax is patient and can be used all over the world. By the way, how is the sale of the house going? One must know that you are serious and are trying to overcome the problems others have caused you. Remember, when the investigations start, they will first investigate those people who have left the business involuntarily. Keep visiting employment agencies and write solicitation letters. They are your insurance for the future.

+++

Everything quiet here. No news, even from the scuttle-butt. Everything is clearly handled internally and our call is ignored. The 'wait and see' attitude which has become the norm for this business is in full swing. Be patient. I am preparing a direct line to "Target". Will inform you immediately when completed.

Sale of house now known to most important connections. I behave like a man who is down and out. Humbled by the knowledge that I have lost. I have canceled our annual ski vacation with the Travel Agent that also has "Target" as a client. Word will get around. I'll make sure that our immediate circle knows that this cancellation is the direct result of financial problems. Nothing will indicate the contrary.

RADICAL PEOPLE'S FRONT FOR AFRICA

number of pages: 2   to: Mr. Voute, Shell Netherlands

19 January, 1990

!!!! FREEDOM FOR BLACK AFRICA !!!!

Again your advertisement, which we had hoped to see, was missing. Sometimes, because of a typographical error, an ad is placed under the wrong heading. Therefore we have carefully searched the entire classified section, but were unable to find your ad. Again, we are not anarchists, we hate war, as you do. But there is no other way for Black Africa. Death will be caused by the weapons we want to supply, but how many lives will be lost if the situation remains unchanged? Decades of suppression have caused more deaths than many a war. The assassination of 6,000,000 million Jews by Nazi-Germany in less than five years is terrible and any right thinking person will abhor it. Compared to that, the hundreds every year in Africa are very few. But that doesn't mean that we should remain on the sidelines and stand idly by. Torture is an everyday occurrence, using the same methods we first heard about in 1945. Probably performed by the same German bullies under the extreme right leadership of Herr Treurnicht. Help us to help Black Africa. We approach you this way to protect your interests as well. It is still a covert operation for the moment. Weapons cannot be purchased by official means. Every country tries to remain neutral. Reagan even protected the leadership and Thatcher continues to do so and Bush is not much better. Weapons and supplies must be smuggled in after purchase on the black market.

Only after victory has become a fact, can we identify ourselves and the names of the fighters and organizations that have helped us. Gerrit van der Veen (Dutch freedom fighter during Nazi occupation — trans.) and his accomplishments against the German tyranny were unknown until May 10, 1945. That is the fate of people who fight the just fight. But during that period, too, there were well-to-do individuals and firms who financially supported the underground. That is what we are asking yet again. Your contribution will remain a secret. As you'll notice, even our phone number is missing from this fax. We will be able to give a full accounting of how we will spend your contribution.

Place a classified ad in the 'Telegraaf' for Wednesday, January 24, under the heading 'Greetings and Wishes' with the text:

"Dear RPFA, I want to talk. S."

Restaurant
Tristan

Proprietaire: Francois le Roi
Zandpad 24
1439 BK Wassenaar
Telephone: ████████
Fax: ████████

To Management Shell Netherlands
ATTN: Mrs. J.A. Sijtsma
Rotterdam

Wassenaar, 20 January, 1990

Subject: Anniversary Mr. J.M. Voute

Dear Mrs. Sijtsma:

Enclosed please find the menu suggestions I prepared for you for next March 10. Please take the time to consult with Mr. Voute. I await your comments and changes and would like to discuss the selection of wines in person with you and Mr. Voute.

With friendly greetings,

le Roi

ATTENTION: Mrs. J.A. Sijtsma
            Headquarters Administration

BRUNEI, January 20, 1990

Dear Janny:

Such surprises in store for the Sijtsma homestead. And you keep telling me that nothing ever happens to you. When the time comes, you know that you can use everything in the apartment that may be of use to you. I mean, there is a pram, a bassinet, and so on. We'll be here for some time and don't feel like we want to have another child while we are here. All right, I probably put the cart before the horse, you're not even pregnant yet, or maybe yes? Anyway, you know I am always a bit impulsive. The lazy life here is starting to grow on me. You may not believe it, but I even have daily help in the household. I don't like it, but one cannot avoid it. The drums pass the message of a new arrival to the village, about two kilometers away, and the next morning there are tens of people on your doorstep looking for a job. You have no peace until you have made a selection. It is practically a duty. Everybody has a girl (they call her 'Ama' here) for the cleaning and it is just not done that you should do it yourself. She is a lovely girl, but very slow. In fact, as soon as she has left, I do it all over again. Ben is one week off-shore and one week at home. The week that he's gone is rather boring. I have gotten to know quite a few people, but you don't make real friends in just a month. I have got to find something to do, because this is no good in the long run. There is rather a lot of charity work here, especially by the ladies of the British contingent. I'll have a look-see if there is anything for me. There are also a lot of guest workers from Third World countries. Rather a sad, poor group, that has left home and hearth for a few dollars per month, so they can send it home and enable half a village to live. Perhaps I can mean something to those people. We're really lucky in Holland. I never realized that before, but now that I'm here, it truly hits home.

This week, under guidance of a long-time resident, we were able to visit a 'longhouse'. That was some experience. First a rather long and difficult trip through the jungle. All of us covered in bug spray, a hat, special high boots, cotton clothes. I didn't have all that stuff anymore, but was able to borrow from one of the ladies. I felt like an intrepid female explorer. I looked like Karin Blixen in "Out of Africa." And hot! We have been on a few trips on our own, but never this far. Our guide has been able to build a relationship with the longhouse over the years. That's why they agreed to receive us. We had all kinds of stuff with us to give as presents, like ball point pens, balls and key rings. A longhouse is built on poles and occupied by several families. Everybody has their own sleeping area. There is a long balcony and all sleeping rooms exit onto the balcony. As soon as we arrived, the women immediately covered themselves with sarongs. Then they rolled out mats for us to sit on. They offered us all a cup of rice wine, but I only took one very small sip. It tastes the way baby vomit smells. An old man sat in a corner, clearly an elder, he looked like he was made out of parchment. We had heard that the different tattoos indicated a brave, but for us horrible, past. You know, it wasn't so long ago that they were still headhunters and nobody is sure whether or not it has stopped. The old man in the corner had tattoos from neck to toes. Who knows how many people he killed in his lifetime. It gave me the shivers. As we left the house we met a young man coming out of the jungle, carrying some Jerry cans. He looked innocent enough, wore a modern T-Shirt and he greeted us with a smile. But he, too, had tattoos that peeked from above his collar. It was quiet an experience. But you can only experience it if you are well-known around these parts. Our guide did a lot of social work for these people. I'd hate to think about meeting one of them when alone.

Further, I passed your best wishes on to Yvonne Staverman and you'll probably hear from her one of these days, because she is indeed scheduled to return to Holland soon. They leave toward the end of February after more than five years in the jungle. I see her rather often, she is nice but suffers from psychological problems. I don't know what her trouble is, but I feel for her. I also discovered that she drinks a lot. Especially when Arie is gone off-shore and she's by herself. If she lived in Holland I would be tempted to advise her to get professional help. Arie is not too happy about it either, I understand. He does not say much, he keeps it all in, but you can notice it when they are together. I try to keep her company, especially during the weeks that Arie is gone. It's up and down. One day she'll appear gay and full of exciting stories and the next day I'll find her crouching in a corner, withdrawn. Most of the time with some sort of drink. I don't know if I should discuss it with Arie. I don't know them well enough to get that involved, but I feel for her. I am glad to hear that your mother is getting better. She's a dear. I sent her a card for her birthday. If they don't steal the stamp at the post office here, it will probably arrive.

I'll stop now.

Greet everybody for me, especially your mother and a kiss for both of you.

Carla

FROM: Administration of Mr. J.M. Voute
TO: Company Security, Mr. B.A. Torenvliet

Number of pages: 4

1/22/90

Dear Mr. Torenvliet:

At the request of Mr. Voute, I am enclosing three faxes from the Radical People's Front for Africa, received during the past weeks.

Mr. Voute wants you to know that there should be no reason for concern. Copies are sent to you as a formality. In case we receive additional communications, we'll forward copies to you.

Headquarters Administration

Mrs. J.A Sijtsma

Attached: 3 faxes from Radical People's Front

RADICAL PEOPLE'S FRONT FOR AFRICA

number of pages: 1   to: Mr. Voute, Shell Netherlands

25 January, 1990

!!!! FREEDOM FOR BLACK AFRICA !!!!

Again we have received no answer. Your pride and self-satisfaction are irritating and devoid of any sense of reality. Your shortsightedness and the self-assured manner of the multi-nationals has again been proven beyond any doubt. Can we only arrange a dialogue by first cutting pipelines, blowing up service stations, or hurting people? Is that the only language understood by the upper management of a multi-national? We don't ask you to agree with our methods in trying to achieve our goals to quickly bring about a permanent and effective change in Africa. But civilized people answer their mail, or, as in this case, a request, a call to arms. A refusal, or a negative answer is your right, ignoring us is an insult. We would like to speak or correspond with you through normal channels. Regretfully that is impossible under the present circumstances. The work that must be accomplished, the help which we are prepared to give, must be done covertly, for the time being. The latent and adversary position of the governments and politicians in question allow us no other options. Overt help with weapons and supplies do not fit in with the present diplomatic set-up. No doubt dictated by the fear of involvement in internal policies. A painful example is the attitude to recent developments in Rumania. We look forward to communicating with you if you really are concerned about the fate of the millions of black Africans. We don't claim to have found the only solution, but we do maintain that the situation, as it has been allowed to fester for decades, can no longer be tolerated by the Western world.

Place a classified ad in the 'Telegraaf' for Wednesday, January 31, under the heading 'Greetings and Wishes' with the text:

"Dear RPFA, want to talk after all. S."

FROM: Administration of Mr. J.M. Voute
   TO: Company Security, Mr. B.A. Torenvliet

Number of pages: 2

1/26/90

Dear Mr. Torenvliet:

Herewith, as promised by phone during your conversation with Mr. Voute, a copy of the fax which we received this morning.

Headquarters Administration

Mrs. J.A Sijtsma

Attached: fax from Radical People's Front

faxbericht/facsimile message

----

aan/to	naam/name	t.a.v./attn.
X5X40X8X92OX8	Amsterdam Police	Mr. Bakkenist

----

van/from	naam/name	ref. no.
X42X89X73804	Shell	Torenvliet

----

aantal pag./number of pages: 3

The Hague, January 26, 1990

Dear Henk:

Our office is receiving some strange faxes lately. Hereby a copy of the latest one. I don't think it means very much, but nevertheless, I'd like to know if you are familiar with the organization mentioned. Taking into account the type of language used, I don't think we are dealing with a very aggressive group. Please let me know at your convenience and best wishes to your family. When will we meet next?

Greetings,

Anton Torenvliet

AMSTERDAM MUNICIPAL POLICE

Headquarters: Marnixstraat

FAX TO:	**ATTN:**	**NUMBER:**	**PAG.**
Shell Security	Torenvliet	~~X756X21X30X268~~	1

Amsterdam, 1-26-90

Dear Anton:

Organization not known to us. Suggest you keep an eye on it. It always starts with the best possible motives, but you never know how it will end. Keep me informed in case you receive more of this not-so-funny stuff.

I'll call you at home tonight to make a date for the near future. Gives us a change to b.s. about our diverse bad guys. The ladies might even enjoy it.

Greetings,

Henk Bakkenist [signature]

Henk Bakkenist

****

No reaction to fax 4 of phase 1. We are 18 days into the schedule and time for harsher words in fax 5. We'll sharpen our tone somewhat, but will count on not getting an answer yet.

We'll have to increase the pressure. Fax 6 will be sent after February 7. It is vital that a recent fact, or event, known only to "Target" will be mentioned. It is of extreme importance to include this in order to be taken seriously by the organization.

Will expect some detail from you on the agreed upon date.

++

In connection with your request I will send you a recent event on the second day of week 6 at 23:30 Dutch time. This fact will not be known at the normal transmission time. I have a good idea what will make an impression. There will be no risks to our organization and I don't even have to identify myself in order to obtain the information. You can count on being able to use the information in your follow-up fax. I suggest that you mention it in passing, as an accidental slip. We must create doubt. The greater the doubt that can be created regarding our organization, the sooner we'll be paid.

TO MRS. CARLA VINK

1 February, 1990

Dear Carla:

I have been unable to write you sooner because I am as busy as a one-armed paperhanger. It is very nice of you to offer your baby things and I accept them gratefully. Meanwhile Frank is busy getting the nursery ready. He practically wakes up with a Black & Decker in his hands. He has also brought home the first sample books for the wallpaper. The first of many, he said. The way things look now, he is certainly not wasting his time. I'm about three weeks late, so who knows. I'll be seeing the doctor next week and we'll know more. You'll be the first to know.

Mother is home again and everything is fine. Surrounded by her friends in the apartment building she has little to complain about. Whenever you go there, there is always somebody visiting. Every night a party! Sometimes I feel I should make an appointment to visit her. But I am glad she is so active. Your card for her birthday arrived and I was asked to thank you. You'll be getting a letter from her. We offered her a trip for her birthday, but she did not want it. Now we are giving her money, because she wants to buy a new car. Would you believe it? 79 years old and a new car. She had to pass a special test for her license, but breezed through it with flying colors. She told me: You now have a DMV-approved mother. She really enjoys life. She started again with old Bert. They share season tickets for the Theater and the Opera and they go at least once a week.

It was a shock what you told me about Yvonne Staverman. She is a bit of a wretch, real pitiful sometimes. I know her well enough and I know a little about her background here, which is not so nice. She has even been under the care of some sort of shrink for a while. I think that your concern will be good for her. She's shy and has an inferiority complex a mile wide. With Arie off-shore it will be especially difficult for her. She is a dear and I am sure that she needs company, but it will be difficult for her to express herself. She was barely 17 when she married him because her father had thrown her out. I am glad that those two are otherwise all right.

In the office everything is 'same old, same old'. Nothing new and a lot of work.

Love from all of us,

Janny

RADICAL PEOPLE'S FRONT FOR AFRICA

number of pages: 1   to: Mr. Voute, Shell Netherlands

1 February 1990

!!!! FREEDOM FOR BLACK AFRICA !!!!

It is clear to us! The multinationals wallow in money, power and self-satisfaction! The only people to which they owe their soul and their loyalty, all work and live at 5 Mint Square. Deaf and blind because of self-overrating, arrogance and self-aggrandizement they look down on what they think of as faceless masses from their modern, glass encased ivory towers. Fascism is now legal and is practiced by well-dressed gentlemen in pretentious director's suites where compassion for others is regulated with the thermostat from the air-conditioning. Where respect and sympathy for the people is hidden in the magnetic strip of the credit card. That's the place where your emotions and feelings are hidden and that's the place where we will hurt you.

We now demand $10,000,000.00 and there will come a time that you will be glad to pay it!!!!

!!!! FREEDOM FOR BLACK AFRICA !!!!

AMSTERDAM MUNICIPAL POLICE

Headquarters: Marnixstraat

FAX TO:	ATTN:	NUMBER:	PAG.
Shell Security	Torenvliet	◼◼◼◼◼◼◼◼◼◼◼	1

Amsterdam, 2-2-90

Dear Anton:

The tone is changing and I am not too happy with that. I would advise you to keep a close look on developments. Would you mind sending me the original of one of the faxes? I'll have it checked out in the lab. I don't think that the boys will find anything, but you never know. Obviously the letters have been written on a pc and those things hardly show any variation in the type. As far as that's concerned, the times of the old typewriters were a lot easier. You could sometimes tell the manufacturer, or model, by a single letter.

Looking forward to tomorrow night.

Henk Bakkenist

HAAGTECHNO, Ltd.

Rietveldenweg 60 / 5222 AS 's-Hertogenbosch   Fax: 🗙🗙🗙🗙🗙🗙🗙🗙🗙🗙

TO: AMSTERDAM MUNICIPAL POLICE / COMMISSARIS BAKKENIST

Den Bosch 02-02-1990

Dear Mr. Bakkenist:

Herewith we confirm that the referenced fax has indeed been sent with the aid of a Panasonic machine, Model UF-130. We have imported about 25,000 of this model for distribution in the Netherlands market. It is a model that is primarily used by small and medium-small sized companies. Also individuals, especially medical people, use this particular model a lot. This model is not recommended for larger concerns, particularly where long documents have to be transmitted. Partly because the document control, including the so-called "log of sent faxes", is limited. The memory can contain just 10 numbers. Another reason for concern, where communications are intensive, to decide against the UF-130. Regarding your question whether or not the reproduction of each machine can be identified by some small deviation: we cannot answer that at this time. We have passed the question on to the manufacturer, Matsushita in Japan, and we will communicate the results as soon as possible.

Hoping to have been of service, I am,

W.J. Hoogstraten

ROYAL DUTCH SHELL
SHELL NEDERLAND

Headquarters Administration   *   **Hofplein**   *   **Rotterdam**

FACSIMILE MESSAGE TO: Restaurant Tristan
ATTN: Mr. Le Roi   NR OF PAG: 1

Reference: Anniversary of Mr. Voute, March 10, 1990

Rotterdam, 2 February, 1990

Dear Mr. Le Roi:

Tentatively, as of this moment there will be approximately 95 guests.
Definitive numbers will not be known until March 2 because of the
possibility that a number of people may still be abroad.

There will, however, be no less than 95 guests.

The menu we discussed has been approved and within a week I will send
you the rest of the program for the evening.

J Sytsma

Mrs. Sijtsma,
Headquarters Administration.

faxbericht/facsimile message

---

aan/to	naam/name	t.a.v./attn.
X3864XX2X36X	The Hague Police	Comm. Vaart

---

van/from	naam/name	ref. no.
XX4X35X80X9X	Shell	Torenvliet

---

aantal pag./number of pages: 8

The Hague, February 2, 1990

Dear Mr. Vaart:

Herewith a number of copies from faxes received during the last few weeks. As I told you by phone, I have already informed commissaris Bakkenist of the Amsterdam Municipal Police.

The "Radical People's Front for Africa" is not known there.

So far it has been established that we are dealing with a simple fax machine, Panasonic, which has been confirmed by the importer, Haagtechno, Ltd. in Den Bosch. We are awaiting further technical particulars from Japan. We will inform you of any further developments concerning this case.

With professional greetings,

Anton Torenvliet

B.A. Torenvliet,
Chief, Shell Company Security

CC: Rotterdam Municipal Police

++

Following information received by telephone: "Target" played tennis with a friend earlier tonight and won 6-4, 6-3.

RADICAL PEOPLE'S FRONT FOR AFRICA

number of pages: 2   to: Mr. Voute, Shell Netherlands

7 February, 1990

!!!! FREEDOM FOR BLACK AFRICA !!!!

We have carefully read the papers in the last few days in the hope of finding an answer from you. Unfortunately we were disappointed, again. In our latest communication we were rather aggressive, which is not usual for us. We would appreciate it if you would consider that fax as not having been sent. Within our organization the opinions of various freedom fighters are sometimes opposed and it is not always possible to express a unified policy to the outside, especially because of the recent developments in South Africa and the imminent freedom of Nelson Mandela. The solidarity within our ranks has been re-established and we can assure you that we are the type of organization that abhors anarchy in whatever form. Of course, we have sympathizers in the Netherlands who can furnish us with information and help us to lighten our load. We know what we are about and before we initiate any action we are fully aware of what we are starting and what the consequences will be. The golden rule in the strategy of war is: Know your opponent! This applies to every conflict or game. With that type of knowledge it is possible to win 6-4 and 6-3 in a tennis match.

Again, we do not advocate anarchy, we do not belong to any political action group, we are a support organization that wants to help the black population of Africa in their efforts to force the white minority, under the leadership of F.W. de Klerk, to see reason as soon as possible. We hope that you understand the humane nature of our efforts. Because we know that a grant of this size cannot be decided by you alone, we will give you seven days to get the matter straightened out within your company. Before your concern transfers the funds we demand, we'll provide you with an inventory of the quantity and type of weapons we intend to purchase with the funds. In case you so desire, we will also provide you with the names of the middlemen and dealers in Libya, with whom we are in contact.

Place a classified ad in the 'Telegraaf' for February 14, under the heading 'Greetings and Wishes' with the text: "Dear RPFA, I want to talk. S.", in

ase you are still discussing the matter within your company. If you come
o an agreement with your Board of Directors, place an ad with the text:
Dear RPFA, (amount) million kisses from S." We will then contact you.

!!!! FREEDOM FOR BLACK AFRICA !!!!

FROM: Administration of Mr. J.M. Voute
TO: Company Security, Mr. B.A. Torenvliet

Number of pages: 2

2/8/9

Dear Mr. Torenvliet:

Herewith the fax we found in our office this morning. Mr. Voute is en-route to Caracas (Venezuela) at the moment. If you want to discuss this with him in person, you'll have to wait until 7 PM, Dutch time.

With friendly greetings,

Headquarters Administration

Mrs. J.A Sijtsma

8 February, 1990

Dear Carla,

Frank has dug out his tools, he has selected the wallpaper and tonight he has cleared out the room.

You know what that means: I AM PREGNANT!!!

How about that! I am a month underway, so we can expect it around the end of October. Everything looks good, but I'll have an amniotic fluid test next week, just to be safe. After all, I am not exactly a spring chicken anymore. I have not yet had the opportunity to discuss it with Mr. Voute, but I'll do that as soon as possible.

Love,

Janny

faxbericht/facsimile message

| aan/to | naam/name | t.a.v./attn. |
| ~~534788X9538~~ | Amsterdam Police | Mr. Bakkenist |

| van/from | naam/name | ref. no. |
| ~~X42988X9328~~ | Shell | Torenvliet |

----

aantal pag./number of pages: 3

The Hague, February 8, 1990

Henk:

Attached is another message from our friendly, local terrorist organization.
It is really starting to bother me. I thought that, in view of the last fax we
received, they might have given up, but that proved to be an idle hope. Mr.
Voute is at this moment somewhere over the Atlantic, en-route to
Venezuela, so I cannot reach him. I have also informed the colleagues in
The Hague and Rotterdam regarding this development.

Greetings,

Anton Torenvliet

Anton Torenvliet

THE HAGUE MUNICIPAL POLICE

Headquarters: Peace Palace Straat

FAX TO:	ATTN:	NUMBER:	PAG.
Shell Security	Torenvliet	XXXXXXXXXXXXX	1

----

8 February, 1990

Dear Mr. Torenvliet:

We received your fax this morning and would like to share our people's discovery with you. Inspector Leener noted that all faxes are sent after 1800 hours. This could mean that one of your employees is using a machine within your firm. This would also mean that with each transmission the person removes the phone number and then re-enters it after use. A rather complicated, but not impossible, operation. It is also possible that the person has a regular job and is only able to transmit from his private address, after hours.

Keep us informed of further developments.

With professional greetings,

a.W.Vaart

Commissaris A.W. Vaart

AMSTERDAM MUNICIPAL POLICE

Headquarters: Marnixstraat

FAX TO:	ATTN:	NUMBER:	PAG.
Shell Security	Torenvliet	X̶X̶8̶3̶9̶X̶8̶5̶4̶6̶8̶	1

Amsterdam, 2-8-90

Dear Anton:

This business is starting to annoy me. The wishy washy tone is even less to my liking than the previous one. I'll have De Berg and Freriks assigned to this for a while. Perhaps there is something known about this organization among the various groups that have picked Amsterdam as a haven. We do have some "canaries" that have relations with some African groups.

By the way, does Voute play tennis?

Greetings,

Henk Bakkenist

INTERNAL FAX COMMUNICATION - SHELL HEADQUARTERS

FROM: Administration of Mr. J.M. Voute
TO: Company Security, Mr. B.A. Torenvliet

Number of pages: 1

2/8/90

Dear Mr. Torenvliet:

At your request I have called Mrs. Voute and related your questions to her. Indeed, her husband plays tennis. His regular tennis night is Tuesday night. The night before his departure for Venezuela he played at the enclosed court (The Hall) of the Country Club in Rijswijk.
The Fax number for Shell/Caracas is + XXXXXXXXXXXXXX.
I hope this information is of use to you.
With friendly greetings,

Headquarters Administration

Mrs. J.A Sijtsma

faxbericht/facsimile message

---

aan/to	naam/name	t.a.v./attn.
X329X526X37X	Shell Caracas	Mr. Voute

---

van/from	naam/name	ref. no.
5X37X2X3X93X8	Shell	Torenvliet

---

aantal pag./number of pages: 3

The Hague, February 8, 1990

URGENT MESSAGE FOR MR. VOUTE
ARRIVING TODAY FROM SHELL NETHERLANDS

Herewith a fax we received today. It has been noted in The Hague that the time of transmission is always after 1800 hours. It is therefore possible that it is somebody who uses one of the machines within the Company, after hours. We do know that the person uses a Panasonic Panafax UF-130, which is not used within the Company. Another aspect is that the sender probably knows that you play tennis. From your wife we learned that you played on Tuesday night, before your departure.

Did you notice anything that, in retrospect, seemed strange to you? Are the same visitors usually there, or does that fluctuate? Did you notice anybody with a peculiar manner, or anybody who suddenly seemed more than usually interested in you? Or somebody who asked questions that, upon reflection, might have led to a certain type of conclusion? Were there any people who obviously ignored you, acted as if they were not interested in you at all? Who was your opponent that night? At this stage we would like the smallest details which may lead to some answers.

As long as you're in Venezuela, we don't foresee any problems, but I would like to suggest that we arrange for some extra protection upon your return to Holland.

With friendly greetings from a cold, grey and damp country,

B.A. Torenvliet

Enclosure: Fax from Radical People's Front for Africa

SHELL S.A. VENEZUELA

* Avenida los Reyes Catholicos - Caracas Cuidad *

FAX PARA: Shell Company Security/Mr. Torenvliet

February 8, 1990

Dear Mr. Torenvliet:

I will only have been in Caracas for a little over an hour, when you receive this fax. I have thought about your questions, but I regret that I'll have to disappoint you. It is usually the same group of people that get together for a set, or so, on Tuesday nights. Most of them I have known for years and the newcomers, or those who show up from time to time, are at least known by appearance. That night I played with an old friend, whose name I can give you, but it seems unnecessary.

I want to share one thought with you. I did win that night with 6-4 and 6-3. Although I know that people in your profession don't believe in coincidences, I think that's all it is. We'll discuss the extra protection you suggest when I return to Holland.

With friendly greetings,

J.M. Voute, Esquire

----

aan/to	**naam/name**	**t.a.v./attn.**
X329X52837X	The Hague Police	Comm. Vaart

----

van/from	**naam/name**	**ref. no.**
X83X72XX93X8	Shell	Torenvliet

----

aantal pag./number of pages: 2

The Hague, February 9, 1990

Dear Mr. Vaart:

Attached is the fax Mr. Voute sent from Caracas and wherein he states that he did win with 6-4 and 6-3 on the Tuesday in question during a game at The Hall, in Rijswijk. The fax from the RPFA (dated 2/7/90) mentioned that exact same score. As Mr. Voute suggested, it may be a coincidence, but it may also be that the sender wanted to give some indication about his information service and that he is very well aware of the whereabouts of Mr. Voute. Do you think that some sort of investigation at the tennis court will be productive?

Greetings,

Anton Torenvliet

B.A. Torenvliet

THE HAGUE MUNICIPAL POLICE

Headquarters: Peace Palace Straat

FAX TO:	**ATTN:**	**NUMBER:**	**PAG.**
Shell Security	Torenvliet	████████████	1

The Hague, 2-9-90

Dear Mr. Torenvliet:

I have issued instructions for an investigation at the tennis court, The Hall, in Rijswijk. We'll ask for a list of all the players on last Tuesday, February 6. It seems desirable to carefully conduct a very discreet investigation at this time. If the person for whom we are looking was there, that night, it might be dangerous to provoke him before we know his identity. I'll let you know of any additional information we uncover.

A. W. Vaart

Commissaris A.W. Vaart

---

aan/to	naam/name	t.a.v./attn.
~~K3204K263?4~~	Shell Caracas	Mr. Voute

---

van/from	naam/name	ref. no.
~~5837283?9068~~	Shell	Torenvliet

---

aantal pag./number of pages: 1

The Hague, February 9, 1990

Dear Mr. Voute:

We cannot ignore the similarity between the score of your tennis game on Tuesday and the score mentioned in the fax sent the very next day. We have informed the police in The Hague, Rijswijk being under their jurisdiction. Commissaris Vaart has promised to conduct a very discreet investigation at The Hall. I cannot shake the idea that the sender <u>wanted</u> to give us some information which would indicate the effectiveness of his organization.

Because you'll be absent from Holland for several weeks, I wonder if it might not be wise to reply in some manner to his request for an advertisement. We could compose a text that will indicate that you are abroad and unable to come to terms with them. It gives us some time for an investigation and will prevent any irritation on their part, which may become dangerous.

They want an answer by the 14th, next.

Please advise.

Sincerely,

Anton Torenvliet

B.A. Torenvliet

SHELL S.A. VENEZUELA

* Avenida los Reyes Catholicos - Caracas Cuidad *

FAX PARA: Shell Company Security/Mr. Torenvliet

February 9, 1990

Dear Mr. Torenvliet:

We will not give in to terrorism in any form. Therefore I am against the placing of an announcement in the paper. I believe that the scores are pure coincidence. It is not that remarkable. The score 6-4, 6-3 happens a lot.

Greetings,

Jm. Voute

J.M. Voute, Esquire

faxbericht/facsimile message

---

aan/to	naam/name	t.a.v./attn.
~~XXXXXXXX~~	The Hague Police	Comm. Vaart

---

van/from	naam/name	ref. no.
~~XXXXXXXX~~	Shell	Torenvliet

---

aantal pag./number of pages: 1

The Hague, February 9, 1990

Dear Mr. Vaart:

I have just received an answer from Mr. Voute and he rejects any idea of placing an ad in the paper. Perhaps it would be a good idea if you convinced him of your point of view. I believe it would be smart to respond in some way, but Mr. Voute has the last word in this matter.

You can reach him at the Fax number below:

SHELL S.A. VENEZUELA +~~XXXXXXXXXXXX~~

Friendly Greetings,

Anton Torenvliet

B.A. Torenvliet

THE HAGUE MUNICIPAL POLICE

Headquarters: Peace Palace Straat

FAX TO:	ATTN:	NUMBER:	PAG.
Shell SA Caracas	Mr. Voute	░░░░░░░░░░░	2

The Hague, 2-9-90

Dear Mr. Voute:

From Mr. Torenvliet I understand that you do not agree with our suggestion to place an answer, according to the wishes of the sender of the RPFA faxes.

I would like to convince you otherwise.

We must not be lulled into a false sense of security by the apparent amiable tone of the communications. This is a well-known pattern. The emphasis placed on the humane aspects of the case is dangerous. What we need is time. This morning a number of my people gained some information at The Hall regarding the Tuesday night in question. It seems that not just tennis players visit the bar. There were a number of "passers-by" who had never before been seen by the owner. It is clear to me that somebody, who knows more about this case, was there that night. Policemen do not believe in coincidence, our experience teaches us differently. Amsterdam is checking with a number of informants regarding this organization and we will continue to follow up at The Hall.

I strongly urge you not to minimize the importance of this case. I most urgently propose that we respond in some way.

I propose an ad along the following lines: "Dear RPFA, I am abroad, please wait for me. S."

Please advise at your earliest opportunity.

Sincerely,

A.W. Vaart

Commissaris A.W. Vaart

SHELL S.A. VENEZUELA

* Avenida los Reyes Catholicos - Caracas Cuidad *

FAX PARA: THE HAGUE MUNICIPAL POLICE / Commissaris Vaart

Caracas, February 9, 1990

Dear Mr. Vaart:

You convinced me. I agree that maybe the right thing to do is to place the proposed advertisement in order to gain time. I will be in South America until approximately the 21st of February. I wonder if the opposition will be patient long enough. If the friendly tone of the messages is no more than a tactic which will eventually result in aggression, we should know within a few weeks.

I would like to be kept informed of your progress in this case. You can discuss day-to-day developments with Mr. Stork.

With friendly greetings,

J.M. Voute, Esquire

J.M. VOUTE, ESQUIRE
REMBRANDT LAAN 3
5690 KM RIJSWIJK
TEL: ██████████████
FAX: ██████████████

10 February, 1990

<u>To Mr. Voute from Holland Please!</u>

Darling:

We heard from the hospital. There's hope! The computer has predicted that a kidney will be available toward the end of the month. I talked to Dr. Ashton and he told me that in his experience, the computer predictions are usually right. It is a sort of relationship between supply and demand that is almost always accurate. It is really unbelievable that a machine will tell you whether or not you are going to live. I called Ron immediately and he jumped for joy. I was there only last night and I was not too happy when I went home. He has become fatter and more bloated since a few days ago. It was terrible to see. He was not feeling well, either, because he had been on the machine the night before. He was such a beautiful boy. But over the phone he was really brave, he has that from you.

I talked to the doctor again and he told me that there are many more demands for kidneys than there are available. When you reach a certain age, you're simply not considered. Terrible, don't you think? And to think that we are now just waiting for some young person, a child still, to smash himself to smithereens on a highway, somewhere in America, or wherever. We wait for that like vultures, like hyenas. It bothers me, but there seems no other way. The Academic Hospital in Leiden has been alerted and will maintain the necessary contacts. In a little while I'll go over to Ron for coffee.

I'll ask again if he would not rather spend the last few weeks with us, but I know the answer already.

He really is courageous. He tries to work on some kind of computer program, something his office cannot solve. He tried again to explain it, but it is all Greek to me. In any case, I am glad he still has some outside interests, otherwise he'll just vegetate and that just makes it worse. Jacqueline has contacted him again. She called on the phone. Oh, I understand it very well, such a child cannot face it. Twenty one years and suddenly you see your friend change into a wreck. We must not judge her too harshly for taking flight. That we never heard from her again is difficult to excuse, but it can be understood. That child was in despair, just like us. That she never dated anybody else from that group, is certainly in her favor.

You never believe who suddenly appeared on the doorstep, yesterday: Annemarie Hutters! She looked fantastic. Everything is going well with them, although Henk has still not found any work. Too old, she said. Forty three and already too old! I believe that the rancor of his dismissal has subsided somewhat. Annemarie told me that Henk finally has been convinced that you had no hand in his dismissal. They want to sell their house in Wassenaar and rent something cheap. Apparently the thought did not seem to bother her. She takes it as it comes and I admire that. She knew about your upcoming anniversary, she heard it from the cleaning lady. She works two days for Thea Stork and one morning per week for Annemarie. I think we should invite them. We always got along well. I believe that it will be beneficial. It is obvious that they won't come because Henk will not be comfortable with his former co-workers, but I think we should make the gesture. It will do them good.

I'll stop now, darling. Will you take it easy? Don't get too excited and make sure you sleep well. I don't want to loose you too. I'll let you know as soon as I have additional news about Ron. I'll kiss him for you.

Love,

Leonie

RADICAL PEOPLE'S FRONT FOR AFRICA

number of pages: 1   to: Mr. Stork, Shell Netherlands

10 February, 1990

!!!! FREEDOM FOR BLACK AFRICA !!!!

Dear Mr. Stork:

We would like to remind you that we have a date for this coming Wednesday. Just because Nelson Mandela, after 27 years of prison, will be freed tomorrow, the 11th, does not mean that the battle has been won!!!!

We fight for an honorable cause, not for personal gain, or to gain power. We hope that, as intelligent human beings, we can come to an agreement that will give both parties the feeling to have accomplished something positive for a people living in fear and under oppression. The text should read: "Dear RPFA, (amount) kisses for you. S."

!!!! FREEDOM FOR BLACK AFRICA !!!!

faxbericht/facsimile message

----

aan/to	naam/name	t.a.v./attn.
X3864X2X36X	The Hague Police	Comm. Vaart

----

van/from	naam/name	ref. no.
X2X35X80968	Shell	Torenvliet

----

aantal pag./number of pages: 2

The Hague, February 11, 1990

Dear Mr. Vaart:

Herewith another fax, received this morning. At first glance there does not seem any news, but the venom is in the beginning this time, not at the end. For the first time the fax is addressed to Mr. Stork, the right-hand of Mr. Voute and his replacement during his absence. They know therefore that Mr. Voute is abroad. A disturbing thought.

Sincerely,

Baton Torenvliet

B.A. Torenvliet

CC: Amsterdam, Commissaris Bakkenist
      Rotterdam, Commissaris Mollema

ROYAL DUTCH SHELL
SHELL NEDERLAND

Headquarters Administration   *   Hofplein   *   Rotterdam

FACSIMILE MESSAGE TO: SHELL SA VENEZUELA
ATTN: Mr. J.M. Voute   NR OF PAG: 2

11 February, 1990

Dear Jacques:

Again a fax from our "friends" which I did want you to see. From Torenvliet I understand that this is not to be taken lightly. As you'll see, the fax has, for the first time, been addressed to me and that means that they know you are abroad. The police and Torenvliet assume that this is just a subtle way to let us know that they know your whereabouts. It has been suggested that we look for an informant within the Company. One wants to obtain a list from the importer of all individuals who have bought a Panasonic fax machine of the type being used and then compare that list with a list of our employees. Seems quite a job, but perhaps it will show results. I'll deal with this from now on.

Keep in touch,

Wim Stork

Wim Stork

THE HAGUE MUNICIPAL POLICE

Headquarters: Peace Palace Straat

FAX TO:	ATTN:	NUMBER:	PAG.
Haagtechno, Ltd.	W.J. Hoogstraten	▓▓▓▓▓▓▓▓	1

The Hague, 2-11-90

Dear Mr. Hoogstraten:

In connection with a current, ongoing investigation I am contacting you regarding a statement made to Shell Security. You mentioned that it might be possible to isolate the purchasers of Panasonic UF-130 machines. I would be obliged if you could prepare a list of individuals who have purchased such a machine. I presume that you have some sort of dealer network and this information can be computerized via a central administration. This touches upon a very serious case and time is of the essence.

Thank you for your time and immediate attention to this important matter.

Sincerely,

A.W. Vaart

Commissaris A.W. Vaart

TTENTION: Mrs. J.A. Sijtsma
   Headquarters Administration

        BRUNEI, February 12, 1990

Dear Janny:

Congratulations! I am so glad for you. I hope that I will be in Holland
or the delivery. I don't know yet when we'll get leave, but it should
be sometime during the Fall. Who knows! I do miss you. They are
all really nice people here, but what gossips! But what do you
want, nobody has any serious business to worry about. All those
women sit around the swimming pool all day, doing nothing. And
it seems there is also a lot of hanky-panky. There are very few
good marriages such as Arie and Yvonne, and us, of course.

don't feel much inclination to get involved in that kind of gossip.
You also notice, after having been here a while, a terrible class
distinction. It is really ridiculous. We're all in the same boat, in the
middle of the jungle, but don't think that the ladies of our men's
bosses will associate with us "common" people. The British
contingent is especially good at that. Actually the British contingent
consists of a series of "cliques" and God forbid they should mix
socially! They hardly greet you, although you cannot avoid
meeting them daily, several times even. No, real friends are hard
to come by, here. That's obvious. It does not bother me, but if you
are sensitive to that type of thing, like Yvonne, you soon feel very
lonely. Personally I think that is her biggest problem, although
she'll refuse to admit it. It will be good for her to return to Holland
soon, because if this is to continue much longer, I predict real
problems. Arie confessed to me once, in a frank exchange, that
she has once tried to do away with herself. It gives me the shivers.
She told me that she has hardly any contact with her parents.
I don't know what happened in that family, but there may be
something wrong on both sides. Her mother writes regularly, but
I understand she does not answer the letters. She has not heard
a thing from her father for at least five years. She told me she
knew Arie just three months when she married him. She was 17
and he was 31. The day after they married they left for Brunei.

65

Apparently he is trying to get a job in Holland. He wants to give notice. A bit hasty, perhaps, because he will not easily find an employer like Shell.

But on the other hand I understand. If he stays with Shell the chances are that they will be sent out again and that could be fatal for her. That's not what he wants. I like him and I feel for him.

In any case, I am going to start something to keep me busy. Starting next week, I'll start a kindergarten for the little ones. Our house is on poles and there is all kind of space underneath. I have gathered all kind of stuff from around the compound and it is shaping up real nice. I'll have about a dozen children. Nothing ambitious, some games, some story telling and so and maybe some reading lessons, you know. Our Antje loves the idea. She feels herself as a princess with a mother as teacher!

Anyway, I look forward to it. I think I will enjoy it. You may not believe it, but the little one is already starting to speak English. She plays all day with English and Dutch children (that's allowed) and she absorbs languages like a sponge. Fantastic, no? I hardly ever leave the compound, because what is there on the outside? At the movies they have only Chinese Kung-Fu movies, so that's hardly worth the bother. I read a lot and in the evening we watch TV. There is also a complete video store with the latest films, so that's all right. It will last our time. At the end of this assignment, we'll buy a nice house in Holland. Planning for that takes a lot of time, too.

I stop now, because I have still a lot to do for my "school". A big kiss for both of you from both of us.

Carla

AMSTERDAM MUNICIPAL POLICE

Headquarters: Marnixstraat

FAX TO:	ATTN:	NUMBER:	PAG.
Shell Security	Torenvliet	░░░░░░░░	1

Amsterdam, 2-12-90

Dear Anton:

I am sorry to have to disappoint you, but there is nobody in our neck of the woods who has ever heard of an organization such as the Radical People's Front for Africa. I have closely studied the recent developments and the case becomes more and more volatile. I think it a good idea to place the proposed ad. The longer we can stall, the more chance there is that they will make a mistake. At least, as long as you are talking, there won't be any tricks, we hope. Recently I have started to wonder if there really is an "organization". There is too much emphasis on phrases such as "we know" and "our informants".

I find that hard to believe. If it was indeed an organization with a number of members, something should have leaked by now. This type of organizations seldom have the required solidarity to prevent all leaks. Search within the Company, it's your best bet!

Greetings, also for Lizbeth,

H Bakkenist

P.S. In order to avoid unnecessary publicity: Have an individual do the placing of the ad and keep Shell out of it, for the time being. Not that I underestimate you, but sometimes the small details are easily forgotten.

HAAGTECHNO, Ltd

Rietveldenweg 60 / 5222 AS 's-Hertogenbosch   Fax: ~~XXXXXXXXXX~~

TO: THE HAGUE MUNICIPAL POLICE / COMMISSARIS VAART

Den Bosch 02-12-1990

Dear Mr. Vaart:

Herewith the list of private individuals who recently bought a Panafax UF-130. The machine is relatively recent, therefore the list is still manageable. If you so desire, we can transmit the information directly to Shell/Computer via existing modems. It will be easy to compare this list with other computerized names for possible matches.

Hoping to have been of service, I remain,

Sincerely,

W.J. Hoogstraten

W.J. Hoogstraten

Caracas, 2-12-90

Darling,

There was no way you could have made me happier. Finally a ray of hope for the boy. If there is anything I can do, let me know at once. I really feel guilty about having to let you cope on your own. I did not look forward to this particular trip. It is as if I had a feeling that something was about to happen. Call me immediately if the operation is advanced. I want to be there. In that case, the business can wait. I am trying to complete everything here as soon as possible, but sometimes these South Americans are just obnoxious. They can always find a reason to delay, or cancel a meeting. Two large meals today and another Holy Day tomorrow. Nevertheless I have managed to get the necessary personnel together for all meetings. They thought it was strange, but I intend to keep to my time table. I keep myself and them at it, because I want to leave a day earlier for Ecuador. If I can speed things up there, as well, I'll be able to return almost a week earlier. But I believe I am getting too old for this job. As soon as Ron has been operated on and everything is under control, I want to leave for the bungalow in Vence.

This terrorist-group thing is starting to irritate me as well. Our own security personnel and the police are not too happy with the case. I don't want to worry you, but I would prefer it, if you were not alone too much. Go and stay with one of your friends, or visit Ron for a few days. Just make sure you avoid a regular pattern, so that a stranger cannot predict your movements.

I think it's nice to invite Henk and Annemarie for the anniversary. I always felt sorry for him. Partly he has himself to blame for his dismissal, but I also feel that my predecessor treated him rather unreasonably, to say the least. You're probably right, they may not come, there is still a lot of hurt and I understand that. Why don't we start by asking them over to the house for an evening? Maybe we can repair the relationship to the point where we can resume our trips to the Wintersport. Those were good days right?

But first the boy, that's most important. You know I am not a praying man, but in this sort of situations, praying seems to come natural.

Darling, I stop now. I'll just walk downstairs to fax this letter. Then it's off to bed, I need it.

I long for you,

Jørgen

THE HAGUE MUNICIPAL POLICE

Headquarters: Peace Palace Straat

FAX TO:	ATTN:	NUMBER:	PAG.
Shell Security	Torenvliet	▨▨▨▨▨▨▨▨▨	1

13 February, 1990

Dear Mr. Torenvliet:

One of our computer experts, Lieutenant R. Wildt, will visit your office with the information obtained from Haagtechno, Ltd. He'll report to you first. Will you take care he is introduced to the right people?

Sincerely

A.W. Vaart

Commissaris A.W. Vaart

++

The relationship with "target" has been restored. Expect invitation for
Anniversary Dinner. Contact restored through wife, at my request. Will be
sure to excel in the games of "old boys" and "renewed friendship".
Certainly gained enough experience in the Company. Look forward to
eventual revenge.

Gossip pipe line is performing perfectly. Light panic within certain circles.
Internal security plus police forces of The Hague and Amsterdam chasing
each other in circles. Nothing to get hold of. Details not available, but it is
an indication of things to come.

Continue!!!!

****

eep relationships open, do not loose sight of the ultimate goal. After more
han a year of intense preparation we are approaching the time of justice.
n eye for an eye and a tooth for a tooth!

hose who have decided the fate of others, who have broken careers and
ves to further glory of themselves, who have climbed the ladder over the
acks of others, will crawl and beg and pay any amount we ask.

tay away from the rendez-vous and do not change your life style, or
abits in any way. Remain in the background. Pay close attention to
ansmission days and times, because a reaction is near and we must be
eady to react in turn. Every detail, no matter how unimportant, of
target's" environment can be important and should be transmitted.

Dr. W.W. STORK

Nassau Laan 14   1590 AB Voorburg

TO NEWSPAPER 'DE TELEGRAAF'

Dear Sir or Madam:

Please place the following ad in your edition for Wednesday, February 14, 1990 under the heading "Greetings and Wishes":

Dear RPFA, I am abroad, please wait for me. S.

You may send the invoice to the above address.

Sincerely,

W.W. Stork

THE HAGUE MUNICIPAL POLICE

eadquarters: Peace Palace Straat

AX TO:	ATTN:	NUMBER:	PAG.
hell Security	Torenvliet	▮▮▮▮▮▮▮▮▮▮▮	1

13 February, 1990

)ear Mr. Torenvliet:

Herewith the names of four people within the Shell rganization who own a Panafax UF-130 machine:

I.F. Haas, Langeweg 23, Den Haag. Department: Foreign Relations. Particulars: None; No police record.

R.A. Andriessen, Mees 5, Delft. Department: Purchasing/ hellshops. Particulars: None; No police record.

I.D. Van Der Kamp, Martinuslaan 63, Voorschoten.)epartment: Administration. Particulars: None; No police ecord.

J.M. Jacobsen, Thorbeckeplein 139, Rotterdam. Department: nternal Auditing. Particulars: None; No police record.

The index marks of the four machines have been :ompared with the sample of the received faxes, as provided y your office. No match was observed.

Summation: The sender will probably NOT be within the Company.

Hoping to have been of service, I am,

A. W. Vaart

Commissaris A.W. Vaart

ATTENTION: Mrs. J.A. Sijtsma
            Headquarters Administration

<u>URGENT !!!</u>

BRUNEI, February 13, 1990

Dear Janny:

In exactly 15 minutes I'll be transmitting an extremely confidential
fax. Will you make sure that you receive this personally, without
anybody else getting a look at it? Unless I hear different, I'll transmit
at 17:10, that's 10:10 Dutch time.

Greetings,

Carla

ATTENTION: Mrs. J.A. Sijtsma
             Headquarters Administration

BRUNEI, February 13, 1990

Dear Janny:

I was with Yvonne until 3 am last night. Yesterday afternoon, around 5, I went to see her and found her in a deplorable condition. Things were not right with her. She was in the kitchen, completely apathetic and almost unreachable. After a lot of cajoling I succeeded in getting her to come with me to my house and I tried to cheer her up. Ben was off-shore as well, so that was no problem. After putting Antje to bed, after dinner, I sat up all night talking with her. After a number of crying sessions, she finally poured out her heart. Apparently the marriage between these two is not so good, after all. They have slept apart for over a year now, and hardly talk with each other.

Arie had an affair with a British woman, here in the compound, but that was not the reason for her unhappiness. She feels guilty about the failure of the relationship. Convinced of her own frigidity, she denies any need for sexual contact. She loves Arie, she says, but as soon as he touches her, she becomes scared and starts hating him. For hours we talked and finally we got to the heart of the matter. Apparently she has been abused by her father from about her twelfth year to the day before her marriage. She claims to have lost all feelings and is scared of everything. The reason for her almost constant depression of the last few months is the imminent departure for Holland. She's afraid her father will visit her and that it will all start again. About four years ago, when they were on leave in Holland, he came by and started to make threats and lewd suggestions.

He knew she was alone at the time and she is deathly afraid that he'll come back as soon as she's alone in the house again. Especially since Arie managed to get the job in Holland, which involves a lot of travel. Arie doesn't know a thing about this affair. She never dared tell him. That's also why she never pressed charges against her father. But apart from all that, she feels guilty about her little sister. That one is 9 years younger than her, 13 years at this time. She's afraid that her little sister is now the next victim. According to her, her mother never suspected anything, or, more likely, did suspect, but was unwilling, or afraid to make an issue out of it. Her room was next to her parents and it seems unlikely that her father could act, without the mother knowing something. He would come to her at least twice a week. Every once in a while, if she came home early from school and the rest of the family was absent, her father would grab her during the day. Nevertheless, she also feels that her mother has failed her. That's why she doesn't want any contact with either of her parents. About every six months, she'll write a non-committal letter, out of a remaining sense of duty, and that's it. She has not heard at all from her father, since his last visit, about four years ago. She feels it deeply and I can imagine. In addition she suddenly realized that during all those years of incest, there was never any love involved. She could have understood if he had cared. But she was merely used. He never was interested in any other aspect of his daughter. It is revolting to think about. You read hints about this in newspapers, or whatever, but it's always distant. Suddenly you are confronted with the facts as they happened to someone you know.

She knows I am writing to you, because she has been planning for some time to press charges, but could never go through with it. Apparently I have become the catalyst that has crystallized her resolve. She is now mainly worried about her little sister. She's been gathering some reports about similar cases and feels that prosecution may result in a favorable verdict. She was never able to say much during the time she was still at home. As you know, incest was a taboo item and probably nobody would have believed her, or so she thinks. After pouring it all out, she became markedly calmer and we agreed that she would stay at my house for the rest of the week. Meanwhile she has decided that she will take definitive steps to prosecute her father and, if at all possible, wants to start proceedings before she even returns to Holland. Although she corresponds regularly with her little sister, she has no idea whether or not the child is being abused. As I said: she knows I am writing this and has given me permission to tell you everything. She will read this letter before transmission. I suggested to her that we ask you to start the preliminary work in Holland. Neither one of us has any idea how to go about it. Will it be possible or you to contact a lawyer to get the ball rolling? There are a number of questions. The most important is: Can Yvonne start proceedings from here and how do we go about it?

Do we contact the local police in Maasland (her address), or the police in Rotterdam, where her parents lived? You understand how afraid she is of his anger. I have advised her not to be alone in the house, when she returns to Holland, as long as he's still free. I will also have to explain the whole thing to Arie next week. I have no idea what the reaction from that quarter will be. I cannot decide if it is better that he hears it from me, or from her. Perhaps we should confront him together. I don't know. In any case, I am glad to be able to help her in some way. She must have been terribly lonely all those years. Still, she has also been very courageous, I think.

We both hope to hear something from you soon,

Carla

Dear Carla and Yvonne:

I received your fax about 15 minutes ago and respond at once.

Yvonne, words fail me to express how your story has touched me. We have known each other for several years, not that we had daily contact, but we had a nice relationship. I remember visiting you on your little farm in Maasland, just two years ago, when you were on leave. By the way, are the repairs, after the fire from last year, going to be completed by the time you arrive next month?

Darling, I really feel for you. When you return to Holland, please remember that I will always be there for you. If necessary you can stay with us, whenever Arie has to travel. Especially if you're afraid of your father.

I agree that this should be turned over to the courts. Not just for you, but also for your little sister.

I can imagine that you worry about her. We read a lot about incest lately. There is quite a lot of information about it in Holland and we have learned that the perpetrator easily switches to the next child, once the first one has left the house. I'll give you all my support and I shall immediately contact an attorney. I know of one, a woman. I met her once, during a dinner with some friends, and I know that she specializes in this sort of case. She is really a nice and caring person and she will be able to give you the proper advice and support. During my years with the Company I have met dozens of lawyers and I feel that I am a pretty good judge of one. Also, she is a woman and for this type of case, it is always easier to talk to a woman, I think. She is very competent and a worthy opponent for the other side. And that's what you need. I'll let you know today.

Janny

Dear Yvonne:

I just got off the phone with the attorney, I could not reach her sooner, because she was in Court. I explained the situation, transmitted your fax to her and gave her Carla's phone number. You can expect a fax from her sometime tomorrow afternoon (your time). Her name is B. De Ridder-Michaelsen, Esquire, Prinses Anna Laan 11 in The Hague. Phone: ✖✖✖✖✖✖✖✖✖✖✖✖✖, Fax: ✖✖✖✖✖✖✖✖✖✖✖✖.

Please don't hesitate to tell me if there is anything I can do. I do worry about your sister. I have the urge to go pick her up from school and to take her home.

What can we do?

Please hang in there and lean on Carla, there is no better friend to be found, anywhere. I know from experience.

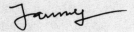

ATTENTION: Mrs. J.A. Sijtsma
           Headquarters Administration

BRUNEI, February 14, 1990

Dear Janny:

We waited for your fax tonight and it just arrived. Before we go to bed, a little update. I thank you from the bottom of my heart for your help. I don't think I could have faced it alone. In retrospect I should have done something a lot sooner. I just don't know what stopped me before. You write about my sister, I do worry about her as well. I know so well what he'll do to her if he cannot control himself. I don't know why it is bothering me more, just the last few months. Perhaps because he did not start with me until I was twelve and subconsciously I have been thinking of her as being too young for sexual contact. But she is 13 already and it worries me more and more.

I don't think that your impulsive reaction to pick her up after school and take her home with you, is strange at all. I wonder if it may not already be too late.

She doesn't know you, but perhaps we can solve that. I could write her a letter to be sent to you by fax and you could give it to her. I can explain things in the letter and also give the reason why you are contacting her. I don't dare write her through normal channels. I am almost sure that my father will go through her mail, before passing it on. In any case, that's how you could get to talk with her. The only problem is: if it's true, what we fear, you can hardly send her back home after that knowledge. Then what?

I can hardly bear to think about it. And do you really think you can pick her up and then hide her? I don't think so. I don't want her to suffer that way, too. Another possibility, and frankly I don't believe it, is that there is nothing going on. Perhaps he has been able to control himself. Then we have different problems. We have then burdened the child with my past, she'll probably talk to my mother, who'll talk to my father. She probably knew, all those years, or worse, allowed it. Just a lot of questions without answers. Another

82

possibility is to talk to the headmaster of her school. They may have noticed something. Perhaps we can approach it through the family doctor. He can maybe call her for a routine check-up, or something. Please understand, I don't have any solutions, but something should be done. Perhaps you'll have an opportunity to discuss this with Mrs. de Ridder?

I have no solutions but the mere fact that I don't know is slowly driving me crazy. The exact date of our arrival in Holland has not yet been set, sometime within the next four weeks, we expect. The thought that she has been, or will be, abused all this time is terrible. It is now 5 pm at your side. Only God knows what that child will have to suffer tonight. Let's hope we can do something about it, fast.

As soon as we hear from Mrs. De Ridder, you'll know about it.

Love from us both,

Yvonne Staverman

Mr. J.K. Goudswaard
Mr. F.W. Goudswaard
Mr. R.E.K. Benckhuyzen
Mrs. B. De Ridder-Michaelsen

ATTORNEYS-AT-LAW
Prinses Anna Laan 11
2509 XT Den Haag

PHONE: ██████████████
FAX: ██████████████

FAX MESSAGE FOR MRS. Y. STAVERMAN; BRUNEI

14 February, 1990

Dear Mrs. Staverman:

Your friend, Mrs. Sijtsma, informed me of your experiences and I have read the faxes between her and you. I can understand your fear that your little sister may have become the victim of incest. Of course, you want to protect her.

In addition, you fear unwelcome attentions from your father, once you return to Holland. Although experience shows that the chance for that is minimal, I can understand your apprehension.

At this time it is important for me to know if you want to institute criminal proceedings against your father, in consideration of past events, or if you want to limit action to taking steps designed to prevent your sister from becoming the victim of your father.

If you want to institute criminal proceedings, you must do so in person, upon your return to the Netherlands.

Before taking that decision, however, I think it desirable if I point certain things out to you.

As you will understand, you cannot remain anonymous during criminal proceedings. You will be asked questions that can become, to say the least, extremely uncomfortable. You will have to relive the entire episode and you'll find that your emotions and feelings will not be respected, or spared.

The pre-trial investigation will be performed by the Judge-Advocate. You will have to appear as a witness, of course. In order to prevent having to appear in the actual case, whereby confrontation with the suspect (your father) will be inevitable, you can request the Judge-Advocate to make a statement under oath. In that case your sworn statement will be sufficient and actual testimony during the court case will be unnecessary.

Nevertheless, it will remain a traumatic experience for you, no matter what the circumstances.

In case you want to limit your actions to taking steps for the protection of your sister, I would advise you to first contact her school. In case incest is committed, it is usually accompanied by a marked change in behavior. I would advise to inform the Headmaster of your sister's school of your experiences and request that extra attention be paid to your sister's behavior patterns.

In case it is suspected that your father is indeed abusing your sister, the Juvenile Protection Act will take effect immediately. A special Juvenile Court Committee will then investigate the situation thoroughly and can advise the Juvenile Judge to remove the child permanently from the household. Your sister will then be permanently placed with foster parents.

Please advise which steps you want to take and I will be available to counsel and advise you.

With most friendly greetings,

B. de Ridder-Michaelsen, Esquire

February 14, 1990

Dear Mrs. De Ridder:

I want to try and tell my story as completely as possible, in writing. My full name is Yvonne Antoinette Staverman-van de Brink. I was born in Rotterdam on February 23, 1968. Father: Gerrit Jan van de Brink, born in Alkmaar on December 11, 1946. Mother: Agnes Verdonk, born in Gouda on April 30, 1948. Their current address is Tulip Square 23 in Delft. I have a sister, Bianca, born on May 18, 1977 in Delft.

My father was always very dictatorial in his manner. Especially toward me. I can remember fearing him, even as a small child. He often punished me. Mother never punished, but threatened with father. Mother used to complain a lot. My mother was (and is) a whiner. We were still living in Rotterdam at the time. We later moved to Delft. I was nine years old at the time. I lived there until I married at age 17. We have been raised in the Christian Reformed religion and used to attend church every Sunday.

The first time my father tried to have carnal contact with me was shortly after my twelfth birthday. We used to have a camper at the time and used to spend the summers on the beach. My sister and I had our own little tent for sleeping. One night, while my sister was away overnight, with some friends who lived in the neighborhood, my father approached me and started to caress me inside my sleeping bag. His hand slipped inside my panties and he tried to insert his finger into my vagina. I resisted. This was also the first time that he took his penis out of his trousers. It was erect. The only other thing I remember about that incident was an indescribable fear. He did not try to approach me any more during that summer. I did not dare to discuss it with my mother, more so because frank and open discussion were not common in our household. Most certainly not discussions regarding sexuality and other, intimate matters. My mother did not explain anything, when I had my first menstruation. I had to discover everything for myself and to this very day I find it difficult to discuss such matters. It is one more reason why I have been unable to discuss this with my little sister and why I am now so afraid for her.

A few weeks after our vacation, I came home from school at about twelve thirty in the afternoon. Mother was at work (she worked half days at that time) and father was at home. We were together in the living room. Suddenly he pulled out his penis and started to masturbate in my presence. It scared me.

Then I had to take his penis in my hand and had to satisfy him. I had to sit on his lap and he kissed me with his tongue, which I found repulsive.

He touched my breasts and sucked them. With one of his hands he felt my vagina. From that day I tried to avoid being home alone with him. I skipped lunch. My sister attended a kindergarten and was not home during lunch. He would punish me if I stayed away from home. Sometimes he would take me into the pantry. But usually he would start masturbating in the living room and then order me to follow him to the pantry. Afraid of his temper and his punishment, I would follow. He would then take his pants off. I had to remove my skirt, or slacks, and while he felt my vagina, I had to bring him to orgasm. Sometimes with my mouth. Although he many times proposed actual intercourse, I managed to avoid that by saying that I was afraid of becoming pregnant. The few times that within my family, in the most roundabout ways, preventive measures were discussed, such as the pill, my father would voice strenuous objections on religious grounds. To this day I have been unable to understand that hypocrisy. During that time I was emotionally tossed between hate and love for my father. For no apparent reason he would sometimes be really nice to me and I could get anything I wanted and just as suddenly he would beat me. The events, as described, would happen once or twice per week. As I got older, I used to attend parties with a girl friend. My father would always pick me up afterward. I was then 15, 16 years old. Before returning home, he would always take me for a ride. I then had to satisfy him in the car. I also remember, that whenever we were home alone, I always had to leave the bathroom door open. The sound of my urinating excited him.

After my father was through with me, I always felt very dirty. Afterwards I would throw up in the bathroom and would thoroughly wash my hands, genitals and brush my teeth.

When I started to date boys, he reacted very strongly. He threatened me by saying that he would always keep me, even if I got engaged, or got married. No boy was any good, according to him. He would become especially violent if I saw a boy who did not belong to our church. Therefore I married Arie within three months after I met him. I don't want to say it was an escape, because I loved him, truly. But the fact that I would be able to leave almost immediately with him to go abroad, most certainly influenced my decision. The night before my wedding day, my father still sought me. This was also the first time he entered me. According to him it did not matter anymore, because I was getting married anyway. Again fear compelled me to let him have his way. I did take a morning-after pill, almost at once. I had to promise father never to discuss the affair with anyone. He threatened to deny everything and I had no witnesses, he said.

I married with the thought (and hope) that everything would now be better. In any case I had escaped my father's influence by going far away. But problems seemed to pile up. At first the life in the compound seemed very nice, but it soon proved otherwise. I was also still very young, barely 17! Everybody around me was older. I had few acquaintances. Partly that was my own fault. I was afraid of close contact. Especially during the weeks that Arie had to work off-shore and I had to remain behind. Sexually, too, there were problems. I have denied Arie a lot. But I have never been able to tell him about my past. In retrospect that was perhaps not too smart. I am sure that he would have been able to understand my fears and he would have been able to slowly lead me to a loving and fulfilling relationship. That too, I saw fail. I started to get physical complaints, such as heart palpitations, shortness of breath, etc. About two years ago my depression led me to an act of despair and I still cannot understand how I came to do it, or found the courage to do it. I swallowed a large bottle of aspirin. Miraculously, Arie found me in time. He had come home two days sooner than expected because of a slight accident at the rig. When I recovered we took early leave and spent a month in Indonesia. I had resolved to tell Arie everything at that time, but again the courage failed me. After that vacation things were better for a while, but for the last year or so my fears and doubts have returned and seems to have grown in strength. I am afraid to return to Holland and start living there permanently. I am afraid of my father. During all the years we have been here, I have not heard a single word from him.

I would very much like you to take all necessary steps to discover if my sister is at risk. I hereby give you the authority needed to contact her school on my behalf and give you permission to have this letter read by the school authorities.

Time is short. She is already 13 years old. She is a cute kid and looks disturbingly adult.

She currently attends the Christian School in Delft. Before that she attended the Rembrandt Grade School.

With friendly greetings,

Yvonne Staveman

RADICAL PEOPLE'S FRONT FOR AFRICA

number of pages: 2   to: Mr. J.M. Voute
Hotel Herradura
Quito Ecuador

15 February 1990

!!!! FREEDOM FOR BLACK AFRICA !!!!

Finally we received a message from you, although it was not the message
we expected. You did not have to tell us that you were abroad, because as
you see, we knew that. We will, this time, respect your reasons, but are
fully aware that this is to your benefit. Despite the fact that we are a
reasonable organization, you must realize that our patience is far from
endless. If we suspect that you are deliberately delaying matters, we will
be forced to treat this matter more severely. You cannot fool us. In case
your request for delay is prompted by the hope that we will make a
mistake, we'll have to disappoint you.

We communicate by fax because we want to remain untouchable.
Telephone conversations can be tapped and correspondence can be
subjected to laboratory tests. The fax is an anonymous communication
method that cannot be localized. Wherever there is a telephone, we have
the means for transmission. The average transmission time is less than a
minute, too short to trace. We will arrive at a point in these negotiations
that will permit you to transmit to us. That has been planned for.

When the time comes, we will give you detailed instructions. For the time
being, traffic will be one-way. We are still the party that sets the terms and
makes the demand and you will have to obey. This is not a threat, but it
could become such, if you delay too long. We fight the good fight to serve
others. For a person with a villa in Rijswijk, a bungalow in Vence and a
limousine with driver this may be hard to understand. But there are still
fools left who will sacrifice their lives for the underdog. In a reasonable
manner we ask you to understand this.

That's the way we work and that's the way we want to continue. Do not
force us to take a path against our will. But please disabuse yourself of the
idea that we are not familiar with other methods, if forced to use them.
Perhaps this would cause sorrow to one of the parties involved. Your
sacrifice is only a small offering compared to the tens of thousand who

can be saved from the clutches of E.F. de Klerk and his vassals. Black Africa needs weapons. You and I know there is no other way.

The time will come when the white minority has to share the power with the black majority. As a token of our goodwill, we will be patient because of your business trip. We'll contact you again.

!!!! MANDELA IS FREE AND AFRICA WILL FOLLOW !!!!

TO: SHELL NEDERLAND
ATTN: Mr. W.W. Stork

QUITO, 2/15/90

Wim:

They know how to find me everywhere. I cannot help but think it is
somebody on the inside, but that's probably no news to you. Send this
along and keep me informed.

The conference is not very important. The results were decided before we
even sat down at the table. Tomorrow is the second session and if it goes
like the first one, I'll probably be leaving a day early for Rio. I don't feel like
sitting here as a sort of glorified marionette for the further glory of a
number of military personnel, probably on their way out already.

Only let me know the most important items, solve the rest yourself. I'll be
leaving in less than three years and you'll be in the hot- seat by yourself
then, anyway.

Greetings, also for Thea,

Jm. Vorile

faxbericht/facsimile message

| **aan/to** | **naam/name** | **t.a.v./attn.** |
| X3864X28X36X | The Hague Police | Comm. Vaart |

| **van/from** | **naam/name** | **ref. no.** |
| X2X35X80968 | Shell | Torenvliet |

----

aantal pag./number of pages: 2

The Hague, February 16, 1990

Dear Mr. Vaart:

It seems our man is aware of the movements of Mr. Voute. Enclosed fax confirms this. Also, the fact that he knows about the family bungalow in Vence (France), proves that he must be an intimate. As Mr. Voute pointed out, he has to be connected with the Company, probably somewhere in Headquarters Administration. The majority of our personnel are not aware of the travels by management. Perhaps the sender is not among us, but at the very least his informant is. There seems no other possibility. The fax reached Ecuador before Mr. Voute did and that gives food for thought. Even the hotel was known. I am at a loss. The people in Headquarters Administration are completely trustworthy with long service records in which they have proved their loyalty to Shell over and over again.

The tone of the last fax has changed yet again. It is no longer friendly and that, too, worries me. In retrospect it was a good move to contact them through the ad. I'll be in my office the rest of the day and await your findings.

Sincerely,

Anton Torenvliet

B.A. Torenvliet

THE HAGUE MUNICIPAL POLICE

Headquarters: Peace Palace Straat

FAX TO:	ATTN:	NUMBER:	PAG.
Shell Security	Torenvliet	XXXXXXXXXXXX	1

16 February, 1990

Dear Mr. Torenvliet:

I share your concern. Perhaps we can start with a list of personnel who were aware of Mr. Voute's trip. No matter who that might be. Through which Travel Agency do you book your trips? Which Janitorial Service do you use? Is everything securely closed and locked at the end of the day? Does Mr. Voute have any personal enemies? Has somebody recently been dismissed, who might be out for revenge? Is there perhaps a connection outside the firm which is not immediately apparent?

All these questions are, I am sure, familiar to you, but I wanted to list them, anyway. I propose that you prepare a plan of attack and then let me have those parts for which we are better equipped.

I'll await your communication with interest.

Sincerely,

A. W. Vaart

Commissaris A.W. Vaart

| **aan/to** | **naam/name** | **t.a.v./attn.** |
| X3864X2X36X | Shell/PR | Mr. Hafkamp |

| **van/from** | **naam/name** | **ref. no.** |
| X24X5X8X988 | Shell | Torenvliet |

----

aantal pag./number of pages: 1

2-16-90

Dear Jules:

Mr. Voute is on a business trip to a number of Latin American countries. In connection with an investigation, the nature of which I am at this time not at liberty to discuss, I would like to know if this trip has been publicized in any way. If so, I would like a copy of the text provided to the media, or a tape. Also a transcript of any, eventual interview to that effect.

Please hurry. Greetings!

Anton Torenvliet

Anton Torenvliet

MR. J.K. GOUDSWAARD
MR. F.W. GOUDSWAARD
MR. R.E.K. BENCKHUYZEN
MRS. B. DE RIDDER-MICHAELSEN

ATTORNEYS-AT-LAW
PRINSES ANNA LAAN 11
2509 XT DEN HAAG

PHONE: ✗✗✗✗✗✗✗✗✗✗✗✗✗
FAX: ✗✗✗✗✗✗✗✗✗✗✗✗✗

FAX MESSAGE FOR MRS. Y. STAVERMAN; BRUNEI

14 February, 1990

Dear Mrs. Staverman:

I regret to have to inform you that your suspicions concerning your sister
are correct.

Today I visited the Headmaster of your sister's grade school, Mr. Doornik,
who told me that a change in Bianca's behavior had been observed
during her last months there. Her tests, also, seemed to have shown lower
grades than could have been expected from earlier scores.

Next I visited the director of Bianca's current school and I talked to her
tutor. Their experiences are disquieting and indicate difficulties at home.
Tomorrow I intend to speak with Bianca. I have made an appointment for
10 AM to meet with her and her teacher will be present, as well.

Would you please be so kind as to send me a fax, addressed to your
sister, in which you explain certain things and introduce me. I will pick up
the fax at my office on the way to Bianca's school.

With friendly greetings,

B. de Ridder-Michaelsen, Esquire

BRUNEI, February 12, 1990

Dear Bianca:

I hope you will not be too scared when Mrs. De Ridder gives you this note. I don't know exactly how to tell you what the problem is. I will leave that to Mrs. De Ridder.

You will probably be upset by what she is going to tell you, but once you have heard her out, you will understand why I had to come to this decision. She may be asking you some very intimate questions that may not be very nice. But you can trust her and you must tell her the truth, no matter how bad. I hope that my fears will be unfounded. If that's so, you'll have to forgive me for mixing you into this business.

If you want to reach me at once, you can phone, or you can write a letter that Mrs. De Ridder will then fax for you.

Lots of love from your "big" sister,

Yvonne

MR. J.K. GOUDSWAARD
MR. F.W. GOUDSWAARD
MR. R.E.K. BENCKHUYZEN
MRS. B. DE RIDDER-MICHAELSEN

ATTORNEYS-AT-LAW
PRINSES ANNA LAAN 11
2509 XT DEN HAAG

PHONE: XXXXXXXXXXXXXX
FAX: XXXXXXXXXXXXXX

FAX MESSAGE FOR MRS. Y. STAVERMAN; BRUNEI

17 February, 1990

Dear Mrs. Staverman:

This morning I had a long conversation with Bianca and it is now certain that she has been forced to submit to sexual abuse by her father. She told me everything in detail, which was a difficult and emotional thing for her to do. After our conversation, which was witnessed by the director of her school, I have taken her to my office. She is very brave and relieved that things are now in the open. I immediately invoked the Juvenile Protection Act and a special representative will be here within the hour. It is to be expected that Bianca, pending a court hearing, will be removed from the household at once. Since foster parents have not been selected and in order to avoid an institution, Mrs. Sijtsma has offered to take her in for as long as needed. Bianca likes the idea. She is still too guilt-ridden and self-conscious to be able to face relatives, which would be the next choice. The final judgement of the Juvenile Court, regarding a permanent foster home, will certainly be delayed for another three or four weeks and it is my understanding that you will be in Holland yourself, by that time. We can then explore the personal aspects of this case.

I am sorry that your suspicions proved to be correct, but we can be thankful to have intervened at this early stage. Attached is a short note from Bianca.

With friendly greetings,

B de Ridder

B. de Ridder-Michaelsen, Esquire

Dear Yvonne,

Don't worry about me. Everything is fine, now. Everybody is really nice to me. I am so glad to have told everything. I am happy I don't have to go home tonight. It is sad for mama, but I think she will understand. I don't want to see papa again.

It is still a long time before you get here. I wish the time would fly. Can I come and live with you, when you're back in Holland? Or are you leaving again?

I tried to write this letter on the computer in Mrs. de Ridder's office and that's pretty hard, but she'll correct it for me.

A big kiss from me,

Bianca

Darling:

I arrived yesterday afternoon in Rio and the first talks are already behind me. My next meeting is at one o'clock with the Brazil Management. I ordered breakfast from room service and thus managed to get a few hours rest until the meeting. I sorted out a number of things during the flight and now have some extra time to write to you. I am already three days ahead of schedule. If everything continues to go smoothly, I'll be back on Tuesday the 21st. It is now about 3 PM at your end. If you have the time, write me back and transmit it around 1 AM. That way I'll hear from you after dinner, before going to bed.

How is our boy? Has the latest news cheered him up? Don't let him lose hope! Easy to say for me, of course, because I am healthy. Sometimes you wonder about the unfairness of life. I am 57, never sick and a wonderful life with you and our son, at 27, is waiting on a kidney in order just to remain alive. I can hardly bear the thought. I have never felt this lonely on a trip before. The games business people play, which have always so fascinated me, have lost their attraction. I function by rote and by routine, but it is almost impossible to be interested. I wonder if I should wait another three years to retire. As soon as I am back I want to have some detailed discussions with Wim Stork about his succession. I'll also do some fishing at the next Board meeting. I am more and more distracted and I feel unable to put out the full 100%. The concerns are too important and this way I am no longer making a contribution to the business. I am tired of it all. The Anniversary on March 10, means nothing to me. Big deal! 25 years with the same firm! Who cares? That's how I think these days.

What if the boy is scheduled for his operation that day? How can I sit there, shake hands and look cheerful? Perhaps we're better off to delay the whole affair until this business is behind us. If you agree, arrange it then with Janny. She'll be able to take care of all the details.

My love to both of you,

Jaap

J.M. VOUTE, ESQUIRE
REMBRANDT LAAN 3
5690 KM RIJSWIJK
TEL: ░░░░░░░░░░
FAX: ░░░░░░░░░░

18 February, 1991

To Mr. Voute from Holland Please!

Darling:

A quick note before bedtime. I think it is a very good idea. I called Janny this afternoon and she'll postpone the festivities until further notice. She discussed it with Wim and he agreed completely, as well. For me, too, it's a relief. I really did not want to get involved with all that at this time.

I have not heard anything from the hospital during the last few days, otherwise I would have told you at once. I'll call again tomorrow. They probably think I am a pest, but they'll have to get used to it. As soon as I know something, I'll let you know. I went shopping with Annemarie Hutters this afternoon and we made a tentative date for an evening at our house, when you get back and are able to arrange the time.

Ron, considering the circumstances, is doing well. As much as possible he works as one possessed. Jacqueline is there every night and that does him good. It is clear that his indifference, when she left, was just an act. He loves her, that's obvious. She is really kind to him. She is a nice child and he is happy. That's all that concerns me right now. Ron's happiness is all that really matters.

Go to sleep and don't get too excited. There are more important matters in life than oil. If you want to take early retirement and we have to make some adjustments, that's fine with me. As long as you're happy.

All my love,

Leonie

ROYAL DUTCH SHELL
SHELL NEDERLAND

Headquarters Administration   *   Hofplein   *   Rotterdam

FACSIMILE MESSAGE TO: Restaurant Tristan
ATTN: Mr. Le Roi   NR OF PAG: 1

Reference: Anniversary of Mr. Voute, March 10, 1990

Rotterdam, 19 February, 1990

Dear Mr. Le Roi:

Mr. Voute has indicated the wish, because of family circumstances, to postpone the Anniversary Dinner till further notice. There is a real possibility that he will not be able to attend on March 10. Therefore, our Board decided to cancel the arrangements for the time being. We will inform the guests. When circumstances change, we will contact you again for a new date. The costs, incurred by this cancellation, may be invoiced to us.

Sincerely,

JSytsma

Headquarters Administration
Mrs. Sijtsma

TO: Mr. B.A. Torenvliet / Security
FROM: Jules Hafkamp
REF:
PAGES: 1
DATE: 2/19/90

Dear Anton:

A very short answer to your question: Apart from a column in the Employee Magazine of January, no publicity of any kind has been connected with Mr. Voute's Latin-American trip.

Greetings,

Jules Hafkamp

++

Phase 3 of our plan involves taking the son of "target" as hostage. That has been decided more than a year ago.

Via the grapevine I learned the following: The son has been extremely ill for more than six months. He has a kidney disease that will be fatal, unless a transplant can be performed. Transplant operation must follow immediately upon the availability of a kidney. Meanwhile the patient is subject to regular kidney dialysis at the Academic Hospital in Leiden.

Has this complication been foreseen?

****

Phase 3 is at least three to four weeks away. Therefore we have the time to decide upon an alternative, if necessary.

The complication is far from minor, but can perhaps work to our benefit. For the time being we'll stick to the original plan. Try to find out on what days he has to go to the hospital. There should be a number of days between each treatment. Because of this extra time limitation, more pressure will be put on them and this may facilitate negotiations.

Kidnapping of "target" is out of the question, because his protection will be too formidable. Other Management members will create too many problems.

Question: Has "Target's" son moved back home?

++

I really question the wisdom of maintaining the original plan under the new
circumstances. A patient is an extra complication during execution of the
plan. Think about special meals, dietary restrictions, etc. Medical
complications are also a possibility. This, apart from my personal, moral
objections to the kidnapping under the new circumstances. An important
aspect of our plan is the prevention of accidents. With this kind of hostage
it is difficult to predict how he will react, physically, to the kidnapping. I
propose looking for an alternative.

****

gain, phase 3 is a long way off. I will consider the objections, but
aintain that negotiations will be less complicated and shorter, under the
rcumstances. After dialysis, a kidney patient should be fine for a number
days. Moral objections are not part of my considerations. I do not want
hear about sentiment or any changes of the plan for the time being.
rovide at once all necessary information.

Dear Yvonne and Carla:

    I am just about ready to leave for Mrs. de Ridder to pick up Bianca. She has been there for a consultation. She has been with us since last Saturday. Somebody from Juvenile Protection has talked to the parents. They'll deliver some things here for Bianca to take care of the next week or so. I look forward to having her here and you can depend on me taking good care of her. One of these days I'll take her to mother, so that she can visit there, too, in case she is lonely during the day. I am also giving her some pocket money, because all she had were her school clothes and her books.

    The amniotic fluid test was OK. Everything is looking good and we are as happy as can be. Frank is very loving and caring, but sometimes he drives me up the wall. I am not allowed to do anything He must think I am an invalid, or something. Last night he started a long lecture about the single glass of wine I drink with dinner Mother calls every day with additional advice. She seems to spend hours looking through women's magazines, finding items about pregnancy and delivery. It is a bit strange to be the center of attention so suddenly. But nice, too.

    Altogether an exciting time and I enjoy it.

    That's all for now, additional news to follow.

    Greetings and love from the three (no, the FOUR!) of us!

Janny

faxbericht/facsimile message

----

aan/to	naam/name	t.a.v./attn.
⟨386⟩4⟨8⟩⟨8⟩36⟨7⟩	The Hague Police	Comm. Vaart

----

van/from	naam/name	ref. no.
⟨24⟩35⟨45⟩⟨8⟩⟨9⟩⟨8⟩⟨8⟩	Shell	Torenvliet

----

aantal pag./number of pages: 1

The Hague, February 19, 1990

Dear Mr. Vaart:

According to our PR department there was, apart from an article in our Personnel Magazine, no publicity connected with Mr. Voute's Latin-American trip. The magazine article did describe the places and peoples he would be visiting in the right order. The hotels were not mentioned, but if we are dealing with an insider, he could have learned that. Generally we use the same hotels for all business trips.

I did start an investigation as a result of the questions you raised, but have been unable to find anything suspicious within the Company. I also investigated the possibility of Mr. Voute having enemies. I talked to Mrs. Voute and she mentioned, in the most circumspect way, the name of Henk Hutters. It seems that Hutters was dismissed from upper management about two and a half years ago. At first this seemed to have been difficult to accept for him and he was very disappointed, according to Mrs. Voute. It has also rankled him that, as of yet, he has been unable to find new employment. Although the two families were very friendly, contact was severed because of his dismissal. The wife of Hutters, however, has renewed contact about a week ago and proposed to find a way to eliminate the misunderstanding that led to the strained relationship. According to the wife, Hutters now realizes that Mr. Voute in no way can be blamed for the dismissal. The Hutters have put their villa in Wassenaar up for sale, but do not seem to be in any financial difficulties. Still, a closer investigation may be worthwhile. The address is 330 Rose Lane. Perhaps this is more your jurisdiction.

Sincerely,

Anton Torenvliet

B.A. Torenvliet

THE HAGUE MUNICIPAL POLICE

Headquarters: Peace Palace Straat

FAX TO:	ATTN:	NUMBER:	PAG.
Shell Security	Torenvliet	❌❌❌❌❌❌❌	1

19 February, 1990

Dear Mr. Torenvliet:

The Hutters family is well known. No police record, debts, or other problems. Mr. Hutters is recorded at the Municipal Employment Agency as "unemployed, looking for work". Apparently he has been very diligent and energetic in his job searches, but has not yet succeeded. No financial problems. No adverse reports from the bank. Has some investments and a small mortgage on the house. No extreme expenses, lives simply. Take a vacation twice a year. No children.

Seems a dead end to me.

We must be patient and look for the first mistake to be made by the Radical Front.

Professional greetings,

a. W. Vaart

Commissaris A.W. Vaart

ATTENTION: Mrs. J.A. Sijtsma
    Headquarters Administration

BRUNEI, February 19, 1990

Dear Janny:

A fax is really a fantastic convenience! I always thought it a bit silly, but no more. Everybody in the compound has one. You eliminate all postal problems. Especially here, the mail is always late, or never arrives.

Everything is fine with Yvonne. I am glad that some action is being taken. She is at home right now, because Arie is supposed to come back today. She has prepared herself for the difficult conversation she will have with him, tonight. After a long struggle she decided she wanted to do it by herself. Alone. I think that's real brave of her. We agreed that, if they felt they needed it, they would both come over here after their talk. I assume she'll write you about the results.

I miss you, especially under these circumstances. I told you, with a few exceptions, the people here are nice, but very superficial. After all, they're only here for the money. I have a nice, lazy life, that's true, but it becomes boring after a while. It is really noticeable that nobody seems to know how to spend all the money they are making. Most of the ladies cover themselves from head to toe with gold. Rolex and Cartier are just brand names. And almost everybody has rooms full of every possible sort of electronic gadget. Ben and I agreed to resist that sort of temptation. I started my little "school" and twice a week I have a dozen children. That's nice for me, as well as for the children. I am starting to become a real "schoolmarm". Your child will be in good hands with me, once we're back.

Do you know if it's going to be a boy, or a girl? Or do you want to keep that a secret? I am really glad for you.

Otherwise not much news. I look forward to one of your letters.

Love from all of us,

Carl

+++

I keep having problems with the execution of the original plan. I don't think that "target's" son should be considered as a hostage. I gained some information regarding the diet of kidney patients in this stage of treatment. It's not so simple. Grain products, milk, eggs, broiled meat in minute quantities, fresh fruit and vegetables as long as they don't contain calcium. There are plenty of other people that can be used instead.

Moral consideration <u>are</u> a factor for me. I have agreed to the plan, support it completely and will do everything possible to make it succeed, but this is different! I cannot agree to keep a seriously ill person as a hostage.

****

Be patient! Time will tell. It depends on the further developments within and the agreements of the organization. Our opponents will eventually decide for us, whether or not we will have to change hostage. We'll sharpen the tone in our next messages to "Target" and we'll start giving the impression that he is the objective. Another two messages are to be sent before the start of Phase 2. Check instruments and equipment.

RADICAL PEOPLE'S FRONT FOR AFRICA

number of pages: 1   to: Mr. Stork, Shell Netherlands

19 February 1990

!!!! FREEDOM FOR BLACK AFRICA !!!!

Mr. Voute will return to Holland this week. We hope that your organization will be ready to discuss with us, in an adult and realistic manner, the help you are to provide for black Africa. The amount is no more than Petty Cash for an organization such as yours. In order to protect your image we have refrained, so far, from making our good intentions public. We are sure, however, that if we were to contact the media, they would immediately take our side in this. Your interests in the South Africa of Botha and De Klerk have been the subject of controversy in the past and you do not have unanimous support from the Dutch population. Nevertheless, we want to bring this affair to a reasonable conclusion, without undue publicity. We sincerely hope that you will not force us to take drastic actions. Taking one of your people as a hostage is not a simple matter, but it is by no means an impossible task for our organization. Don't force me to make that decision. Until now I have been able to convince the members of our organization of your readiness to negotiate in good faith. If it develops that harsher steps must be taken, I will lose my influence. The hardliners in our organization will then take over and nobody will be able to predict the consequences.

Place an ad in the Telegraaf for 22 February under the heading "Greetings and Wishes", indicating your response in the usual manner.

---

aan/to	naam/name	t.a.v./attn.
X3864X2X367	The Hague Police	Comm. Vaart

---

van/from	naam/name	ref. no.
X2435X80988	Shell	Torenvliet

---

aantal pag./number of pages: 2

The Hague, February 20, 1990

Dear Mr. Vaart:

Herewith a copy of the fax which was found in the office this morning.

The new factor is the mention of a hostage. This really makes me uneasy. It is not certain which persons are being targeted, but the fact that Mr. Voute returns this week, may be an indication. I propose to place an ad to try and delay matters. Please advise on the text to be used. A copy of this has been sent to your colleagues in Rotterdam and Amsterdam.

Sincerely,

B.A. Torenvliet

---

aan/to	naam/name	t.a.v./attn.
X3864X2X367	Hilton Rio	Mr. Voute

---

van/from	naam/name	ref. no.
X2435X50988	Shell	Torenvliet

---

aantal pag./number of pages: 2

The Hague, February 20, 1990

Dear Mr. Voute:

Herewith a copy of the fax which was found in your office this morning. They are starting to talk about a kidnapping and I am very uneasy about that. I will station one my people in your house and institute the usual precautions upon your return to the Netherlands. I also want to respond to the request for an ad. We shall compose the text after consultation with the police in The Hague. I will keep you informed.

Sincerely,

Anton Torenvliet

B.A. Torenvliet

TO: Shell Security
    Mr. Torenvliet

    URGENT!!!!

Rio, 2/20/90

Mr. Torenvliet:

This is really starting to annoy me. Please contact my wife and act
according to your judgement. Keep the advertisement noncommittal, make
no promises, but indicate some sort of hope. I'll be back in Holland the day
after tomorrow. Will arrive on KL 383, ETA 13:55.

Sincerely,

J.m. Voute

J.M. Voute

Darling:

Quickly a note about a rather bothersome business. Torenvliet, from Internal Security, will contact you today to discuss plans for stationing one of his people at the house for extra security.

The organization which has been pestering us for some time, is changing from demands to threats. No need to worry, but we should be careful. That way, I'll worry less, too. I'll be back on the 21st and should be home around 3 PM. I'll be on KL 383, so you can check the latest info. Don't come to pick me up, I'll be met.

I look forward to being home again.

Love and kisses,

Jacque

Dr. W.W. STORK

Nassau Laan 14   **1590 AB Voorburg**

TO NEWSPAPER DE TELEGRAAF

Dear Sir or Madam:

Please place the following ad in your edition for Thursday, February 22, 1990 under the heading "Greetings and Wishes":

Dear RPFA, would love to talk. How can I reach you? S.

You may send the invoice to the above address.

Sincerely,

W.W. Stork

+++

"Target" has acquired extra protection, according to the grapevine. A guard from Internal Security has been permanently assigned to the house. "Target" is expected back around 1600. Will be picked up at the airport under heavy security. So far no news about other steps. The case is getting more critical. Phase 2 is approaching. Has a decision been reached regarding an alternate hostage?

****

Extra caution is advised. Change of hostage has been denied. There is no other possibility. Extra security of all possible alternatives creates too great a risk. Want the following up-to-date information regarding "Target's" son:

Still living at same address?
Days and time of treatment at the hospital?
What extra precautions to take at rendez-vous?

RADICAL PEOPLE'S FRONT FOR AFRICA

number of pages: 1   to: Mr. Voute, Shell Netherlands

24 February 1990

!!!! FREEDOM FOR BLACK AFRICA !!!!

Your answer has both delighted and disappointed us. The fact that you are inclined to talk, is good. That you ask how to reach us, however, indicates that you severely underestimate our organization. You cannot reach us! We will also not telephone you. The reasons have been made abundantly clear in previous messages to you. We are not stupid. We know about the possibilities of traps and other dangers and are prepared for everything. As soon as you agree, we'll accept that as a "gentlemen's agreement" and will then tell you how to transfer the funds. Do not try to set a trap for us, however, because that will be doomed to failure. Again, I repeat: do NOT provoke us! As leader of our group, I can only control certain elements within our organization if you cooperate.

Place an ad on Wednesday, February 28 in the usual manner. No more games!

!!!! FREEDOM FOR BLACK AFRICA !!!!

THE HAGUE MUNICIPAL POLICE

Headquarters: Peace Palace Straat

FAX TO:	ATTN:	NUMBER:	PAG.
Shell Security	Torenvliet	░░░░░░░░░░░	1

26 February, 1990

Dear Mr. Torenvliet:

Continuous threats seem to have become a part of the pattern. I would advise to make some sort of concession at this time. The initiative will then shift again. They will then have to reveal a means for two-way communication. Up to now, from an investigative point of view, communication is a dead end. Everything is one-way and we cannot get a starting point. I noticed that the latest fax was transmitted on a Saturday night. That would indicate an individual, transmitting from his house. That is not much help, but maybe another piece of the puzzle.

Sincerely,

A.W. Vaart

Commissaris A.W. Vaart

Dr. W.W. STORK

Nassau Laan 14   **1590 AB Voorburg**

TO NEWSPAPER DE TELEGRAAF

Dear Sir or Madam:

Please place the following ad in your edition for Wednesday, February 22, 1990 under the heading "Greetings and Wishes":

Dear RPFA, I want to give you millions of kisses. Tell me how? S.

You may send the invoice to the above address.

Sincerely,

WimStork

W.W. Stork

TO MRS. CARLA VINK

Rotterdam, 2/26/90

Dear Carla:

I talked to Mr. Voute yesterday and we agreed that I would start working half days in about three months. He was very happy for me and his wife, too, called right-a-way. They are truly nice people. He has become very old during the last few months. He has changed, ever since his son became ill. From one day to the next these people have been confronted with a big burden. In addition, he has to worry about the business, which is a job and a half. As a final straw he has been pestered with some sort of terrorist group for the last few months. Every few days we receive a fax from an organization that, as far as I am concerned, has picked him as a target. He remains rather calm, but I cannot help but cringe at the thought that somebody may be out to do him harm. We have had this sort of threat before and you never know what to expect from this type of lunatics. He is such a nice man. If at all possible, I intend to stay until he retires. That's about three years from now. I discussed it with Frank and he agreed. My mother is already looking forward to the baby-sitting.

Otherwise everything is normal. I am busy and Frank is working on a special project which requires a lot of overtime. Thus, we mostly meet in bed. The child is growing and I am starting to show it. I know what it is going to be, but won't tell you. That's going to be a surprise for everybody. I bought a book with all sorts of baby names and I am having a terrible time of it. The names are either far fetched, sound crazy, or remind me of people I don't like. Mother tries hard to find out whether it is going to be a boy, or a girl, by proposing one name after another. So far, she has not been able to get it out of me.

Bianca is just fine and it is wonderful to have her in the house. She is doing very well in school and when I come home, she has done the shopping and sometimes even the cooking. Frank loves her too. I hear all kind of stories, because Yvonne calls her almost everyday. Boss Shell will love that telephone bill! I keep in contact with Mrs. De Ridder, but the final decision of the Juvenile Court is going to take some more time. For the time being everything is under control and as soon as Yvonne is back, she can help her sister. It would be a wonderful solution if Bianca could stay with her. At least, Bianca, looks forward to it.

That's all for now, back to the salt mines for me. I'll write again, soon.

Love,

Janny

+++

Son of "target" still at same address. Not alone in the evening. He goes to the hospital three times per week for dialysis. He reports to the hospital at 11PM and spends the night there. No extra precautions needed at rendez-vous. Just adjustments for diet.

Question advisability of this action.

****

Plan will remain in force, as is. It was agreed that I would be in charge and I will also take all responsibility. If we are careful, there will be no accidents. End of discussion.

faxbericht/facsimile message

---

aan/to	naam/name	t.a.v./attn.
X3864X2X367	The Hague Police	Comm. Vaart

---

van/from	naam/name	ref. no.
X2435X80968	Shell	Torenvliet

---

aantal pag./number of pages: 1

The Hague, March 5, 1990

Dear Mr. Vaart:

We placed the required ad on 2/28/90 and so far have not had an answer. I don't think that's a good sign. Especially since our text indicated compliance. I have meanwhile increased the protection of Mr. Voute and have assigned personnel to other important management members. This silence bodes no good. I hope they'll be smart enough not to start anything, but you never know. I will inform you as soon as I have more news.

Sincerely,

Anton Torenvliet

B.A. Torenvliet

THE HAGUE MUNICIPAL POLICE

Headquarters: Peace Palace Straat

FAX TO:	ATTN:	NUMBER:	PAG.
Shell Security	Torenvliet	░░░░░░░░░░	1

5 March, 1990

Dear Mr. Torenvliet:

Have all editions of the "Telegraaf" been checked? A newspaper publishes multiple editions during the day and although the difference is only supposed to affect news stories, sometimes ads do not appear in all editions. If they read the ad, you should have heard something. I agree that this is cause for concern.

Sincerely,

a. W. Vaart

Commissaris A.W. Vaart

faxbericht/facsimile message

---

aan/to	naam/name	t.a.v./attn.
X3864XX2X36X	The Hague Police	Comm. Vaart

---

van/from	naam/name	ref. no.
X2X3X4X0X88	Shell	Torenvliet

---

aantal pag./number of pages: 1

The Hague, March 5, 1990

Dear Mr. Vaart:

All editions have been checked. Ad was placed in all editions. By the way, just received a telephone call from one of their reporters. The strange wording of the ad attracted his attention and he reached us via Stork, who has placed the ads in his name. I have been able to stall him for the moment, but feel that is only a temporary measure. We certainly cannot use any publicity at this time.

I propose to wait one more day and then place the ad again. Perhaps this is their first mistake.

Sincerely,

Anton Torenvliet

B.A. Torenvliet

----

aan/to	naam/name	t.a.v./attn.
X3864X29367	The Hague Police	Comm. Vaart

----

van/from	naam/name	ref. no.
X2435450988	Shell	Torenvliet

----

aantal pag./number of pages: 1

The Hague, March 6, 1990

Dear Mr. Vaart:

Seven days and no reaction of any kind. I think that our "friend" did not see the ad. Why not? If the paper was sold out, it is always possible to get a copy somewhere. So that cannot be the reason. Even if he had forgotten the date, it is always possible to check back at the office of the paper.

Another possibility: They have discontinued the action. I don't believe that.

Third possibility: The sender is out of the country. The paper did not arrive for that particular day.

Question: Which country did not receive the paper on that day?

Awaiting your answer,

Anton Torenvliet

B.A. Torenvliet

THE HAGUE MUNICIPAL POLICE

Headquarters: Peace Palace Straat

FAX TO:	ATTN:	NUMBER:	PAG.
Shell Security	Torenvliet	▓▓▓▓▓▓▓▓▓▓▓	1

6 March, 1990

Dear Mr. Torenvliet:

One of my people was able to prove your theory. He checked all the transmission dates as well as the reaction time between ads and responses. There was always a day difference. It would be logical to assume that a response would be transmitted on the day the ad appeared. That has never happened. There was always a day's delay. This could indeed prove that the paper was not available, because it had not arrived yet. A Dutch paper is always a day late in other countries. That is to say, countries not in the immediate neighborhood. That could prove your theory. We checked with Schiphol Airport and found that there was a wild-cat strike of ground personnel on the 28th. Therefore a number of destinations did not receive the paper for that day. When that happens it is not the practice to send the papers a day later, because they will be too much out-of-date. An investigation is under way to find out exactly which countries did not receive papers that day.

Conclusion: We have to take into account that the sender is indeed abroad. Although that cannot be determined from the fax. As soon as I hear more, I will inform you.

Sincerely,

a.W. Vaart

Commissaris A.W. Vaart

Amro Bank   FAXBERICHT/FACSIMILE MESSAGE

NAAM/NAME	T.A.V./ATTN:
Mr. W.W. Stork	XXXXXXXXXXXXXXXXX

VAN/FROM	
J. van Ginkel	AMRO, THE HAGUE

DATUM/DATE	HANDTEKENING/SIGNATURE
6 March, 1990	

Dear Mr. Stork:

In order to bring you up to date, we want to give you a summary of the options that will be due on March 26, next.

				quotation +/-	
Open/Sell	50 put	Philips	APR 50	34.25 -/-	f 157,500.00
" "	100 put	KNP	APR 100	87.10 -/-	29,000.00
" "	50 put	Ahold	APR 140	125.00 -/-	75,000.00

Total NEGATIVE (Debit)   f 361,500.00

We request that you arrange for a deposit of f 360,000.00 (three hundred and sixty thousand guilders) to decrease the margins created by above negative results.

Sincerely,

J. van Ginkel

J. van Ginkel (director)

faxbericht/facsimile message

---

aan/to	naam/name	t.a.v./attn.
X3864X1X8367	The Hague Police	Comm. Vaart

---

van/from	naam/name	ref. no.
X2X35X1X8968	Shell	Torenvliet

---

aantal pag./number of pages: 1

The Hague, March 6, 1990

Dear Mr. Vaart:

If that is indeed the reason it would also mean that the "organization" has no members in the Netherlands. If they did, a reaction to the ad should have been received. Is it possible that we are dealing with a completely foreign organization, perhaps with a Dutch correspondent? If that's true then the entire "humane" purpose, to help black Africa, is no more than a farce. It is now clear why Amsterdam could not find any trace of this organization.

What do you think?

Anton Torenvliet

B.A. Torenvliet

****

For security reasons not all details of action have been told to you. One detail can now be revealed. I asked "Target" to place an ad in the Telegraaf of February 28. I did not receive that particular paper. Get hold of that issue and look under "Greetings and Wishes" for an ad beginning with the text "Dear RPFA". Deviate from transmission schedule and inform me tomorrow at the same time.

++

Text in Telegraaf of 28 February:

Dear RPFA, I want to give you millions of kisses. Tell me how? S.

****

Received information. Thanks. Phase 2 will now start.

Check again and make sure all notes and faxes have been destroyed. There must not be any notes, or whatever, left. We cannot be too careful.

At 8 o'clock tonight proceed to the Bayberry Street in Voorburg. There is a three-story apartment building, starting with number 36. There is a row of garages behind this building. The key, which you received from me at the time, will fit on the door of garage Number 4. Make sure you are not seen and that the parking area is empty before approaching the garage. Wait, if necessary. In the garage you will find a bronze Toyota. You will find the keys on top of the right front tire. Take the car to Schiphol Airport and park it in Lot Number P3, as close as possible to Slot F2. Leave the parking ticket in the car.

TO MRS. CARLA VINK

Dear Carla:

I simply must write you a quick note, because something terrible has happened. Henk Hutters was killed about eight thirty last night. It was murder. It happened in Voorburg. He went to a garage there, where an old car was parked. Apparently the car exploded when he tried to start it. Parts of a bomb have been found and also part of the detonator mechanism. Nobody knows why he went there. It is a complete mystery. Everybody here is going crazy. There are some indications that the incident is somehow connected with the terrorist letters that have been received here for the last few months. But I cannot believe that Henk Hutters could possibly be involved in that. Annemarie went to the hospital to be treated for shock. She is in bad shape. The garage has been completely obliterated. They called me at about quarter past ten to come to the office and I have spent the night here. The police went through everything. In a little while they will close off the floor, move the telephone lines and we'll be moving to another floor. It is a real panic.

I have to leave soon, but I had to tell you.

Love,

Janny

THE HAGUE MUNICIPAL POLICE

Headquarters: Peace Palace Straat

FAX TO:	ATTN:	NUMBER:	PAG.
Shell Security	Torenvliet	▓▓▓▓▓▓▓▓▓▓	2

8 March, 1990

Dear Mr. Torenvliet:

Herewith the copy of the fax which we found in the machine of Mr. Hutters, during a search of the premises.

It is sickening. It is now clear that Hutters was involved in some kind of underhanded affair and after having served his purpose, has been eliminated. He was lured, or told to go, to the garage in Voorburg and so signed his own death warrant. It seems he was no longer useful and knew too much.

His correspondence and other paperwork are being carefully investigated, but so far nothing has been discovered. Finger prints belong to Hutters, his wife and a cleaning lady.

Of course, we keep under advisement the possibility that he may have been connected to the Radical People's Front for Africa, but nothing has yet been discovered to prove a connection. Laboratory tests of the fax are useless because a totally different letter type has been used.

I'll keep you informed,

a. W. Vaart

Commissaris A.W. Vaart

When you enter this room in the course of your investigations you will find this message.

We can assure you that you will find nothing!

Hutters is dead and will not talk any more.

I wish you strength and wisdom.

THE HAGUE MUNICIPAL POLICE

Headquarters: Peace Palace Straat

FAX TO:	ATTN:	NUMBER:	PAG.
Shell Security	Torenvliet	███████████	1

8 March, 1990

Dear Mr. Torenvliet:

Herewith a synopsis of our progress. Further investigations have uncovered that Semtex explosives were used, connected via a detonating device to the ignition key. The car was a 1979 Toyota. The license tags had been removed, but after checking the engine and chassis number we discovered that the car has been listed as stolen since last October. The garage is owned by a Mrs. Schoolen who lives in one of the apartments at number 42. Last year she placed a "TO LET" ad for the garage in a local advertising paper. Last October (note October again) somebody called and rented the garage that same evening for a year. He paid cash in advance. She has not seen him since. She remembers a man of about 35 years, casual, but neatly dressed. Jeans, sport shirt. She did notice he was very tanned. She even asked him if he had been on vacation. She has never seen him since, but it is certain that it was NOT Hutters. She cannot see the garage from her flat, so she cannot say whether or not he visited the garage with any regularity. Although she does have a spare key, she has never been in the garage after she rented it out. She provided us with a name and address which, after checking, turned out to be false.

We did investigate in the neighborhood, especially among owners/renters of other garages, but the outcome is negative. It is clear that the car had been parked there during some night, prepared and then left to be used just once for the purpose of blowing somebody away. Further investigations have established the fact that the car must have been left for several months. The battery was new and was bought in October (!!!) 1989. This certainly indicates that somebody knew that the car would be standing there for some time before being used for this murder at a distance. The perpetrator wanted to make sure that there would be sufficient power to set off the detonation device. It also means that this murder was planned and they knew the intended victim. If this theory proves to be correct then it is certain that Hutters was involved in some sort of nefarious activity. That, in addition to his unsavory Shell past, might indicate a connection to the People's Front for Africa. In any case he had a fax machine. The fact that we still have not received any response to our latest ad, is another suspicious circumstance.

I'll keep you informed,

A.W. Vaart

Commissaris A.W. Vaart

RADICAL PEOPLE'S FRONT FOR AFRICA

number of pages: 1   to: Mr. Voute, Shell Netherlands

9 March 1990

!!!! FREEDOM FOR BLACK AFRICA !!!!

We rejoiced at your reaction in the Telegraaf of February 28 last. It seems we did not make a mistake in choosing our partner. Please forgive the unfriendly tone we have used from time to time. We assume that you agree with our goals. We want to re-emphasize that we keep in close contact with a number of highly placed black Africans who will play an important part in the new Africa. They will be informed of your help and support and your loyalty will be suitably rewarded. We will prove to you that we are friends and once the new administration has taken over, we will not forget old friends. We are NOT aggressive. We abhor the methods of the IRA and the PLO. We do not want to make innocents the victims of our idealism. The terrible murder that happened in Voorburg, only yesterday, is not the means by which we want to obtain out goals. We know that the victim is an ex-employee of your firm, but do not be tempted into the wrong conclusions because of that. We can assure you that you will find nothing to connect us with the unfortunate victim. We want to talk with you and as reasonable people come to an agreement.

We will contact you again, soon.

145

---

aan/to	naam/name	t.a.v./attn.
XXXXXXXXXXX	The Hague Police	Comm. Vaart

---

van/from	naam/name	ref. no.
XXXXXXXXXXX	Shell	Torenvliet

---

aantal pag./number of pages: 3

The Hague, March 10, 199

Dear Mr. Vaart:

Herewith a copy of the fax found in our office today. It is a nice story, friendly, sympathetic, but I don't believe a word of it. It is him!

Please note the text and compare that with the fax you found in Hutters' study. The next to last sentence is identical to the second sentence of the "Hutters" fax: "We can assure you that you will find nothing ..."

Coincidence seems unlikely. Everybody has his/her own ways of saying things. Except when one is a literary expert, perhaps. But subconsciously we all use certain phrases and we all have certain speech patterns that can identify us. I am certain that we are dealing with the same group. Convinced of our knowledge of the situation an attempt is now made to use it to their benefit. Make a strong point from a weak position. By pointing toward yourself you may hope to claim innocence.

It is of course possible that this type of "hint" has been included on purpose. It seems to me that if they are really guilty of the explosion, it might have been more effective to claim responsibility. But they don't do that because are afraid of a more drastic response from our side which might destroy the eventual goals they have set themselves. Hutters had to go, that was certain. They want to remain innocent, however, in order to lull us into a false sense of security. But as far as I am concerned they have betrayed themselves with this peculiar use of words.

Perhaps you can get an opinion from a specialist?

Sincerely,

Anton Torenvliet

B.A. Torenvliet

Enclosure

ATTENTION: Mrs. J.A. Sijtsma
             Headquarters Administration

BRUNEI, March 10, 1990

Dear Janny:

I waited a little with this letter in order to give you a chance to get over the worst shocks you have had lately. It is terrible. I have seen Hutters but once, but I know his wife quite well. I like her. I don't know if I should write her. I find that always so difficult in these circumstances. Of course, I read it in the papers and it was even mentioned on Radio Holland World Broadcast. Do they know yet what he was doing in Voorburg? From what I have been able to gather, it was a messy business. Where terrorists involved? Just don't let it bother you too much. In your condition that is no good. The compound buzzes with all sorts of theories, but nobody really knows for sure, of course. Suddenly everybody knew him, you know what I mean.

You probably heard from Bianca already. Arie and Yvonne Staverman are leaving for Holland tomorrow. Yvonne was so glad that the date had finally been set. She has been lonely, of course, and she also wants to see her sister.

She asked if you would call Leni, you know, the cleaning lady who also works for Thea Stork. I think she also worked one day a week for Annemarie Hutters. Anyway, Yvonne wants to clean the whole house from top to bottom and she would like some help. As you know, their farm house in Maasland was partially burned, last September. A contractor repaired it and according to the neighbors everything is ready. But you understand, contractor-clean and housewife-clean are two different things. Arie cannot help her too much, because he will have to start his new job almost immediately. I don't know if she will want regular help, after that, but she can arrange that herself with Leni, when the time comes. Will you do it?

Otherwise there is little to tell. I had my "class" today and enjoyed every moment. I am dead tired. The questions don't stop and Antje between all those little ones is dearer than ever. She acts as a sort of second teacher. So cute. Anyway, tiring but very, very fulfilling.

Love for both of you from all of us and, of course, also for Bianca. Tell her that I will miss her big sister a lot.

Carla

P.S. Do you know Yvonne's address in Holland? Here it is, just to be sure: Zandweg 18, Maasland. Telephone XXXXXXXXX. Give her a ring sometimes. I don't know why I write this. Bianca knows it, of course.

THE HAGUE MUNICIPAL POLICE

Headquarters: Peace Palace Straat

FAX TO:	**ATTN:**	**NUMBER:**	**PAG.**
Shell Security	Torenvliet	░░░░░░░░░░	1

10 March, 1990

Dear Mr. Torenvliet:

I checked your theory with one of our experts, a psychologist who specializes in this kind of cases. He confirms your theory. I think it only normal caution to assume that we are dealing with the same organization. We must then also take into consideration that they will be capable of any action and will use anything in order to achieve their stated goals. I am also more and more inclined to think that the entire People's Front for Africa is no more than a front, as you mentioned once before. The developments in South Africa are going in a totally different direction and make the views of the Front moot. Yet, they continue in the same vein and that makes it unbelievable. We must remain alert. They'll probably wait with the next actions until this latest incident has blown over a little and we have given this, in their minds, less priority. That's the danger point.

Sincerely,

a.W. Vaart

Commissaris A.W. Vaart

faxbericht/facsimile message

---

aan/to	naam/name	t.a.v./attn.
~~X320182637X~~	Shell Caracas	Mr. Voute

---

van/from	naam/name	ref. no.
~~58372889368~~	Shell	Torenvliet

---

aantal pag./number of pages: 4

(PERSONAL & CONFIDENTIAL)

The Hague, March 10, 1990

Dear Mr. Voute:

Herewith three copies about the Radical Front. I urge you not to take this matter lightly. Hutters has most likely been killed by this organization. We have no leads and even with the help of three police forces, we seem unable to get a lead of any kind. Meanwhile I want to propose that we move the fax machines to a secure area, only accessible to trusted personnel.

I realize that the fax number, in view of normal communications, cannot be changed, but this will limit access to the machines.

Right now almost everybody is able to see and read fax messages. We should change this as soon as possible. The technical staff can convert Room 315 very quickly and a special lock is a matter of minutes. My department will provide a permanent guard. A special pass should be issued to persons authorized to use the space and times will be noted carefully.

I hope you'll agree.

Sincerely,

Anton Torenvliet

B.A. Torenvliet

faxbericht/facsimile message

---

aan/to	naam/name	t.a.v./attn.
X3864X2X36X	The Hague Police	Comm. Vaart

---

van/from	naam/name	ref. no.
X2X36X80986	Shell	Torenvliet

---

aantal pag./number of pages: 1

The Hague, March 10, 1990

Dear Mr. Vaart:

This afternoon the fax machines will be moved to a secure area. Just a few trusted personnel will have access to the machines. This measure has been taken in order to insure usage control. We will have to contact our Insurance Company, The Federal Insurance Company in London, who carry the risk for kidnapping and sabotage. We can also use the professional help offered by this company. As you may know, they are able to draw upon the resources of Ackerman & Palumbo, Inc., a private investigation and security company. This firm has the necessary know-how and contacts that may be of use to us. Although I am aware that A&P uses less conventional methods, I am sure that they will conform to our wishes and ethics in this matter.

Sincerely,

Anton Torenvliet

B.A. Torenvliet

THE HAGUE MUNICIPAL POLICE

Headquarters: Peace Palace Straat

FAX TO:	ATTN:	NUMBER:	PAG.
Shell Security	Torenvliet	░░░░░░░░░░	1

10 March, 1990

Dear Mr. Torenvliet:

I want to make sure that you are aware of the fact that
Ackerman & Palumbo, Inc. is by law prohibited from
operating on Dutch territory. I am familiar with the outfit
and their methods. Of course, you are free to use their
services, if you so desire, but I am not happy with the
thought. I will agree to cooperate under the sole condition
that Dutch laws and customs will be respected.

Sincerely,

A.W. Vaart

Commissaris A.W. Vaart

RADICAL PEOPLE'S FRONT FOR AFRICA

number of pages: 1   to: Mr. Voute, Shell Netherlands

13 March 199

!!!! FREEDOM FOR BLACK AFRICA !!!!

About two months ago we first contacted you and now the time has come
to act. In your latest ad you indicated your sympathy for our goals and now
we want to negotiate the amount with you and also the manner in which
we will be able to take possession. Everything is ready from our side,
therefore you would be well advised to take immediate steps to comply.
From the very start we have mentioned an amount of $5,000,000.- and we
want to go with that figure. At a certain point, during our negotiations, there
was some irritation within our ranks and the amount was doubled. Within
our organization I have been able to reduce this demand to a reasonable
amount. This is proof that I am still in command and the more radical of
our members are not able to influence the final decisions. This is of prime
importance to you. It seems an ideal situation for both parties and it is now
up to you to decide whether or not this amiable situation will continue.

Place an ad on Friday March 16 in the usual manner with the text: "Dear
RPFA, shall we correspond? S."

faxbericht/facsimile message

---

an/to	naam/name	t.a.v./attn.
3864828367	The Hague Police	Comm. Vaart

---

an/from	naam/name	ref. no.
2435480988	Shell	Torenvliet

---

antal pag./number of pages: 1

The Hague, March 13, 1990

Dear Mr. Vaart:

Herewith another copy of a fax, received just minutes ago. It is noticeable that this is the first fax which has been sent in the morning. I will ask Mr. Voute if he agrees to the placing of an ad.

Sincerely,

B.A. Torenvliet

THE HAGUE MUNICIPAL POLICE

Headquarters: Peace Palace Straat

FAX TO:	ATTN:	NUMBER:	PAG.
Shell Security	Torenvliet	▓▓▓▓▓▓▓▓▓▓	1

13 March, 1990

Dear Mr. Torenvliet:

I would most urgently advise Mr. Voute to place the required ad. They want to start corresponding. That means two-way communication. I wonder how they plan to do that. If it indeed comes to some sort of correspondence, we'll be rid of this fax traffic, which is pretty pointless from our point of view. Perhaps this will be the long awaited turning point in the case.

Sincerely,

A.W. Vaart

Commissaris A.W. Vaart

FROM: Administration of Mr. J.M. Voute
TO: Company Security, Mr. B.A. Torenvliet

Number of pages: 1

3/13/90

Dear Mr. Torenvliet:

Your arguments and those of Mr. Vaart in The Hague have convinced me. Herewith you have permission to place the ad. I have also informed Mr. Stork.

Greetings,

J.M. Voute

TO MRS. CARLA VINK

Rotterdam, March 13, 1990

Dear Carla:

Life is getting back to normal. You would not believe the uproar we have had. It is really too terrible, all the things that happened. Annemarie is home again and I went to visit her. She cannot stop talking about it. She has no idea what Henk might have been involved with. She never noticed anything peculiar. Sometimes he was late coming home, or he would stay late in his study, but that does not necessarily make you suspicious. It must be terrible to be confronted with something like that. We have all been interrogated by the police and now there is extra security in our department. The faxes have been moved to a secured area and, apart from myself, only a few people still have access to them. We received a special pass for that purpose. It is expected that the organization that has been after Mr. Voute for several months now, is going to become really threatening. It is also generally assumed that Henk Hutters was somehow connected to them. But no proof has been found. As you know, he was removed from management, some years ago, under less than auspicious circumstances. This apparently counts heavily against him. Rancor, or even revenge, may have been one of his motives. I have been interrogated, too. They even contacted Frank's boss to get information about Frank. It gives you the shivers, but I understand that they want to investigate all possibilities. After several hours with one of those detectives in a little room, you really do start to feel like a suspect. But anyway, the situation is again more or less normal, so I have time for this letter.

Yesterday I went to Schiphol Airport with Bianca to pick up Arie and Yvonne. It was really touching. We went right away to Maasland to drop off the luggage and after that we went for a bite in Rotterdam. They were dead-tired and we agreed that Bianca would stay with me for a few days longer. Also, because the house in Maasland is only partially furnished. Next week she has a semester break and then she'll move in over there.

As per your request, I called Leni and she has contacted the Stavermans. I just talked to Yvonne and she told me that she is going to the police this afternoon, with Mrs. de Ridder, to file a complaint. She sounded relieved. It is really obvious that she had a rough time. The talks with Arie seemed to have been beneficial. In the airplane to Holland she finally managed to tell the whole story. She was still upset because of that, when she arrived. We just let things go, for the time being, also to spare Bianca. Things are difficult enough for the child.

Otherwise everything is fine. The nursery has been painted and papered and we'll be looking for furniture and so, this week. I will stay on the job for as long as possible. I feel I owe it to Mr. Voute. He is not well. He has suddenly grown old. Not physically, but in his behavior. His active and spirited manner is gone. They are still waiting on a kidney for his son. That's all that seems to concern him.

All in all some worrisome times in the office.

Greetings to your man and love from us all,

Janny

**fax from arie and yvonne staverman /
fax number XXXXXXXX**

Maasland, 14 March

Dear Carla:

Yesterday I went to the police with Mrs. de Ridder in order to file a complaint. It was terrible. I had prepared myself for it, I thought, but it is really not very nice. Thank God, the case was handled by a female police officer. If it had been a man, it would have been just that much harder. I understand that my father has been brought in tonight for a preliminary interrogation. I have not heard anything yet from mother. To me that is proof that she must have known from the beginning. I don't want to condemn her, because it is possible that he threatened her as well. If that proves to be the case, I'll contact her again. For the time being, neither Bianca nor myself, are in any need of a reconciliation. I was so happy when I saw her at the Airport. I suddenly realized that I have ignored her too much, when I was still at home. I hope that the Juvenile Protection people will give permission for her to come and live with me. Arie has a job here, now, and it does not look like we are going to be doing a lot of traveling in the future.

Tonight I'll be going to visit Janny and Bianca because Arie is already on the move for his new job. He had to start right away. Yesterday he connected the fax, therefore I can write you so quickly. The thing had been stored in the shed during the last few months in Brunei, which was a bit of a bother. I finally had the courage to tell Arie everything. I have laid awake nights over that, I don't mind admitting. His reaction was rather violent. I knew that, because he is rather volatile. That's why I was afraid to tell him at home, because it would have been too easy for him to lose his temper. I told him everything during the trip to Holland, which had the advantage that he had to control himself. He had calmed down by the time we arrived. I thought that was rather clever of me. We hardly discussed anything else during the trip as you will understand. He was very angry and also very sad and said he would remodel my father's face at the first opportunity. I had to promise that I would file a complaint, but I had already decided that. I really felt sorry for him. With all his anger I could not help but notice that he loves me. Everything that has been a barrier between us for the last few years will now soon be forgotten. We both want this marriage to work. He now understands everything and

I now understand that his affair was merely platonic and nothing more. It was my fault in the first place. We are starting a new life and we want it to be a success. Our little farm house is fantastic and I cannot tell you how happy I am. You have been absolutely wonderful to me during the last few months. It was written in the stars that you would arrive in Brunei during December and that I would find you. It happens so seldom that one meets somebody who can be both loved and respected. I will miss you, I can tell you. You helped me cross some very difficult bridges during the last year. I had lost all courage to do anything about it. It was a terrible feeling. Everything seemed too difficult, too hard, too formidable and yet, with your help, it all became manageable. I have found my sister again and she'll come to live with me next week. I am so happy and I don't know how to thank you. For years I had not met a normal person and I had totally given up all hope. And then you came.

I will write you whatever happens.

Greetings and lots of love,

Yvonne

RADICAL PEOPLE'S FRONT FOR AFRICA

number of pages: 1   to: Mr. Voute, Shell Netherlands

16 March 1990

!!!! FREEDOM FOR BLACK AFRICA !!!!

We rejoice in your cooperation and we will let you know the means for contacting us. As you will understand, we will have to remain under cover for a while. Therefore you will have to follow our instructions.

We assume that you have agreed to the amount of $5,000,000.- (five million dollars) as stated in our last message. The amount must be paid in cash in small, used bills as follows:

American Dollars	$ 1,860,000
German Marks to a value of	1,120,000
Swiss Francs to a value of	1,320,000
Dutch Guilders to a value of	700,000
Total	$ 5,000,000

Take steps to have the amounts available within five days. Our first contact will happen as follows:

Tomorrow night at exactly 23:00 you will receive a fax with just a phone number. You must send your answer within 10 seconds to the number provided. Your answer may not exceed 100 typewritten words. Drawings, signatures and handwritten messages are not allowed. You must use a fax machine with a CCITT Group 3 compatibility. This is to make sure that transmission will not exceed 45 seconds.

!!!! MANDELA IS FREE AND BLACK AFRICA WILL FOLLOW !!!!

THE HAGUE MUNICIPAL POLICE

Headquarters: Peace Palace Straat

FAX TO:	ATTN:	NUMBER:	PAG.
Shell Security	Torenvliet	░░░░░░░░░░	1

16 March, 1990

Dear Mr. Torenvliet:

I wonder how they plan to do that. They must betray themselves when they release the phone number. I will be in your office tomorrow evening and depend on you to keep a number of lines free. I will also inform the Phone Company and arrange for computer tracing of all calls in and out of your building during that time. What I particularly noticed, apart from the fact that this fax was also sent during the morning, was that they reacted on the day the ad appeared in the paper. Even more remarkable, they reacted at 9:02. The paper had barely been on the street for a few hours. This confirms our theory that the previous faxes were sent from abroad. Now that action is near, they have settled in Holland. Let's spend the day to compose a suitable answer. Do please, also consult Mr. Voute.

Sincerely,

A.W. Vaart

Commissaris A.W. Vaart

RADICAL PEOPLE'S FRONT FOR AFRICA

number of pages: 1   to: Mr. Voute, Shell Netherlands

!!!! FREEDOM FOR BLACK AFRICA !!!!

◼▨◼▨◼▨◼-▨◼▨◼▨◼◼

164

RPFA:

We sympathize with the goals of your organization and will have the required funds ready by March 20, 1990.

You have, however, promised us an accounting of the sums and for what and by whom they will be spent. You have also promised the name of the middlemen in Libya. You understand that I have to account for these sums in some way. Ready for further negotiation.

J.M. Voute, Esquire
Managing Director

THE HAGUE MUNICIPAL POLICE

Headquarters: Peace Palace Straat

FAX TO:	ATTN:	NUMBER:	PAG.
Shell Security	Torenvliet	░░░░░░░░░	1

18 March, 1990

Dear Mr. Torenvliet:

Herewith a synopsis of our findings at Lusthower, Inc. at 3 Field Way in Zuiderveld with phone number ░░░░░░░. After contacting the local police from your office, minutes after the number was traced, the local police arrived within 12 minutes at the address. We are dealing with a small firm, specializing in cattle feed. It is rather isolated on the outskirts of the village. A window in the side of the building had been broken in order to gain access to the office. Some footprints and tire tracks have been found. Nobody has seen anything. Our fax correspondent knows what he is doing and has taken all the proper precautions. The closest police station is in Zwolle.

I think that this will be a foretaste of his way of communicating. Of course, he must have researched a number of this kind of addresses and he will have a wide choice available.

The police will always be too late, because he will never have to wait more than 90 seconds for an answer.

I will send a message to all police posts with a description of our experiences, but don't expect any results. The surprise and the initiative will always be on his side. It is impossible to guard all isolated localities in Holland.

It is, however, essential that we remain in contact. We must try to delay matters in order to gain time.

Greetings,

A.W. Vaart

Commissaris A.W. Vaart

RADICAL PEOPLE'S FRONT FOR AFRICA

number of pages: 1   to: Mr. Voute, Shell Netherlands

19 March 1990

!!!! FREEDOM FOR BLACK AFRICA !!!!

You must trust us. Of course, we will be able to give a full accounting as to how your money will be spent. Don't, however, force us to reveal this at short notice. Your questions show ignorance and an extreme lack of knowledge about the way such business is transacted. We will be able to keep our promise only after the weapons have been delivered to the designated recipients. You must not ask us for names, or further details, at this stage of the proceedings. That is impossible. If we were to comply with your request, we would endanger our own people. We must not underestimate the resources of our middle men and an unpleasant reckoning of accounts cannot be ruled out. As soon as this affair is behind us, we hope to be able to disappear into anonymity. Only then will the time have come to acquaint you with the details you request.

Tonight at 23:00 you will receive another phone number and you will have 10 seconds to respond.

RADICAL PEOPLE'S FRONT FOR AFRICA

number of pages: 1   to: Mr. Voute, Shell Netherlands

!!!! FREEDOM FOR BLACK AFRICA !!!!

XXX-XX233

RPFA:

Understand your objections, but hope you will understand the difficulty of my situation. We are discussing a considerable amount and I cannot dispose of this alone. I need the permission of the complete Board of Directors. So far I have only been able to request the bank to assemble the specified amounts. That too, is less simple than assumed. Such amounts are not readily available in cash. A number of banks are cooperating in this effort. You asked for the money by the 21st. I must ask for several days grace.

J.M. Voute, Esquire
Managing Director

THE HAGUE MUNICIPAL POLICE

Headquarters: Peace Palace Straat

FAX TO:	**ATTN:**	**NUMBER:**	**PAG.**
Shell Security	Torenvliet	▓▓▓▓▓▓▓▓▓▓	1

20 March, 1990

Dear Mr. Torenvliet:

The firm in Kessel (phone number ▓▓▓-▓▓▓▓) has been searched by my people last night. Again nothing has been found. The situation is identical to the former case. Isolated and far from any other structures. Also a small firm where entry is easy. No guards. I am certain that the writer transports his own fax and connects it on the spot. A simple process. Again, the nearest police station was 17 km away. The bird had flown long before we could be on the scene.

This will become a prayer without end, I think. I don't know yet how we can turn the situation to our advantage, but if this continues it will soon become pointless. Perhaps we should try to come to a definitive agreement as to the place where the money is supposed to be turned over. Perhaps we have a better chance at that time. Somebody will have to show up!

Greetings,

A.W. Vaart

Commissaris A.W. Vaart

fax from arie and yvonne staverman /
fax number XXXXXXXXX

Maasland, 20 March

Dear Carla:

I finally found some extra time to write you again, since we got back. For the first few days Leni and I have been working like horses to clean all the accumulated dust and dirt. Bianca helped as well. They were wonderful days. Not that I am obsessed by neatness, but you can see the results so quickly, so gratifying. Also, I had not been here since the fire. The contractor did excellent work. Of course, there are a few details I would have changed, but that happens when you're not on the spot. They made a real effort to clean things but, you know, it just wasn't right. Leni is a jewel, she works hard and yet, it is always fun to be around her. She is so typical for someone from The Hague. A big mouth and an even bigger heart. And yakking! And everyday she would bring a cake, or something "for the coffee". I engaged her on a permanent basis. Twice a week a half day. Not because I need the help, but Arie wanted that so. That's another side of his character. I have to be the lady of the house. We also bought new furniture, because a lot was burned, or damaged from the water. For now it is still a bare house. We only have some camp beds and we bivouac in the kitchen. Bianca has a mattress on the floor. In a way it is a lot of fun. The old furniture was bought in our poor period, but the new furniture is really nice (and expensive). It is an ill wind that blows no good. I can hardly wait to see how it will look, but delivery is at least five weeks away.

I also see Janny regularly. When I told her that I would be writing to you, she asked me to give you all her love. So, consider that done. She is very busy. Apparently there are all sorts of problems and complications that make her job harder. But she is very happy with the expected baby.

After we filed the complaint, my father has been interrogated and then set free again. I don't understand that. But according to Mrs. de Ridder this was to be expected. Apparently no repeat is expected because I have moved out and Bianca has also been removed from his influence. It does gnaw a little that I still have not heard a thing from my parents. Bianca is not too happy about it either, but she does not talk about it. I'll let it go for now. In any case, she is very happy with the decision of Juvenile Protection that allows her to stay with me for the time being. We'll be visiting the High School, here in Maasland, this week so she will not miss too many classes.

Darling, greet everybody for me and write me sometime. A big kiss for you both.

Love,

Yvonne

faxbericht/facsimile message

---

aan/to	naam/name	t.a.v./attn.
X3864X2X36X	The Hague Police	Comm. Vaart

---

van/from	naam/name	ref. no.
X2X36X60X68	Shell	Torenvliet

---

aantal pag./number of pages: 1

The Hague, March 20, 1990

Dear Mr. Vaart:

This morning I met with Mr. Voute and a number of other members of Management to discuss your proposal. Your proposal cannot be taken lightly. So far nobody has been taken hostage, there is no indication that they want to exert this type of pressure and we have maximum protection for all key people. Why should we decide to pay? Who can guarantee that this will be the only instance? If it turns out to be this easy to force us to pay, they'll be back again and again. If we then refuse, they would still be able to take drastic action, including kidnapping, or worse. In other words: it is just a stay of execution. In addition there is another complication: Our insurance company (Federal Insurance Company) will not pay out unless there is bodily harm.

An idea was proposed this morning, which has my support.

We will make an agreement with the organization for payment. Instead we deliver a suitcase filled with worthless paper. This will give your people the opportunity to arrest the suspects. If it fails, however, we must count on increased danger as a result of our provocation. We must then increase protection of likely hostages even more, which would include drawing on the resources of the various police departments. Perhaps this is the only way to force a confrontation. In any case, there is no real difference with the situation to be expected if we simply hand over the money.

Awaiting your answer,

B.A. Torenvliet

RADICAL PEOPLE'S FRONT FOR AFRICA

number of pages: 1   to: Mr. Voute, Shell Netherlands

20 March 1990

!!!! FREEDOM FOR BLACK AFRICA !!!!

A nice try, be we know that trick. The supposed permission from the Board of Directors is a real joke. Those people have been informed from the very beginning regarding our demands. Your statement that banks have trouble getting the required amounts together is another piece of nonsense, but we will give you the benefit of the doubt. We will be flexible, but we expect the same from you. We have warned you before: DO NOT force us into actions against our will, which both parties will later regret. We have people within our organization who are not adverse to anything. Some, I regret to say, look forward to harsh action. These are people trained to torture, disable and kill. I am still in control. I continue to convince them of the correctness of my actions. Don't give them a chance. I will not be responsible for the consequences.

Tonight at 23:00 you will receive a new phone number and you can answer us there within the usual 10 seconds. Consider your proposals and do not underestimate us. Our patience is not endless.

RADICAL PEOPLE'S FRONT FOR AFRICA

number of pages: 1   to: Mr. Voute, Shell Netherlands

!!!! FREEDOM FOR BLACK AFRICA !!!!

▓X▓2-X▓4▓▓

PFA:

u should know that matters are settled. The Board of Directors has also
reed. The bank called this afternoon to confirm that all funds have been
llected. There is a small adjustment. There is less than $1,500,000 in
merican dollars available. I have made up the difference in Dutch
ilders. We now await your instructions regarding delivery of the funds.

M. Voute, Esquire
anaging Director

THE HAGUE MUNICIPAL POLICE

Headquarters: Peace Palace Straat

FAX TO:	**ATTN:**	**NUMBER:**	**PAG.**
Shell Security	Torenvliet	░░░░░░░░░░░░	1

21 March, 199

Dear Mr. Torenvliet:

Again a small firm. This time in Langkerk. After investigation not much news to add to the previous cases. Method identical.

Your contemplated action will have to be your sole responsibility. I can agree with your decision in general, bu I think the risk is too high. You can be sure that you will provoke them needlessly which will result in consequences nobody is ready to face.

But I realize that this may be the only way in which we can arrive at a solution. We are forced to react. The whole case has been well prepared and they may be too fast for us.

I have assigned a number of capable officers and the required equipment exclusively to this case. I will also keep in contact with my colleagues in Rotterdam and Amsterdam

Sincerely,

A.W. Vaart

Commissaris A.W. Vaart

RADICAL PEOPLE'S FRONT FOR AFRICA

number of pages: 1   to: Mr. Voute, Shell Netherlands

21 March 1990

!!!! FREEDOM FOR BLACK AFRICA !!!!

our instructions are as follows:

onight at 23:00 you will receive a fax with an address. At the address you
will find a red Ford Escort with a portable phone in the trunk.

Only one person may enter the car, the suitcase with money must be
placed on the seat next to the driver. The left side door may not be locked.
The driver must not be armed and must come alone to the agreed upon
rendez-vous. We will know immediately if you have informed the police.
The driver may not be a police officer, or somebody from Shell Security.
This automatically excludes Mr. Torenvliet.

Don't try any funny business. We know most of your people and Mr.
Torenvliet in particular. The driver must follow exactly the instructions
provided via the portable phone. This particular phone will only receive.
The driver will not be able to talk to us. The instructions will be given just
once. In case a piece of information is missed and the wrong instructions
are followed, we will take that as provocation and the entire exchange will
be cancelled and the consequences will be your responsibility. Perhaps
you should bring a piece of paper and a pencil to make notes.

The driver must leave immediately, after receiving the fax tonight.

Amro Bank FAXBERICHT/FACSIMILE MESSAGE

NAAM/NAME	T.A.V./ATTN:
Mr. W.W. Stork	██████████████

VAN/FROM	
J. van Ginkel	AMRO, THE HAGUE

DATUM/DATE	HANDTEKENING/SIGNATURE
21 March, 1990	

Dear Mr. Stork:

According to your instructions we hereby confirm a futures contract i
your name to the value of US$ 1,500,000 (one million, five hundred thousan
U.S. dollars) for delivery on September 1, 1990 based on an anticipate
value of f1.90 (one guilder ninety cents).

We request that you confirm this order in writing at your earliest convenience

Sincerely,

J van Ginkel

J. van Ginkel (director)

CKERMAN & PALUMBO, INC
ONDON

O: SHELL NETHERLANDS   **FROM:** HEAD OFFICE

ear Sirs:

Mr. John Clark will arrive Rotterdam Airport via BA 173 at
5:00 local time. He will wear a grey hat and carry the Financial
imes in his left hand.

ours Sincerely,

RADICAL PEOPLE'S FRONT FOR AFRICA

number of pages: 1   to: Mr. Voute, Shell Netherlands

!!! FREEDOM FOR BLACK AFRICA !!!!

The red Ford Escort is parked in the Parking Garage on Eisenhower Lane
in slot 23. The key is in the ignition. Drive to Rotterdam Central Station and
wait for instructions.

ROTTERDAM MUNICIPAL POLICE

Headquarters: Liberty Square

FAX TO:	ATTN:	NUMBER:	PAG.
Shell Security	Torenvliet	X3372XX3X478	1

----

22 March, 1990

Dear Mr. Torenvliet:

The red Escort has been carefully searched. It was stolen about three days ago in Amsterdam. Apart from the portable telephone in the trunk, there was another, hidden transmitter, locked to send, behind the dashboard. Everything said in the car could be heard by the opposition. When Mr. Stork transmitted his route via the walkie-talkie, they heard him and immediately cancelled the exchange. Although I figured on some such strategy, I did not consider it wise to let Mr. Stork leave without some sort of communication. I felt the risk was too great to let him go thus unprotected and unguarded. The result is the same. Now they will react to this course of events, otherwise they would have reacted to a suitcase full of worthless paper. Also, the delivery itself, was subject to considerable risk. It is possible that they would have forced Mr. Stork to open the suitcase before letting him go. The consequences would have been even more serious. We have achieved what you hoped and we must now be doubly alert for a different approach.

I understand that Mr. Clark has taken it upon himself to follow Mr. Stork. I want to draw your attention to the fact that such a course of action is extremely dangerous and I have been forced to charge Mr. Clark with obstruction of justice and illegal possession of a firearm. Needless to say, in this type of operation we can do without this sort of "help". I hope you understand my position.

Sincerely,

A. Mollema

Commissaris C.A. Mollema

CC: Comm. Vaart, Den Haag

FROM: Administration of Mr. J.M. Voute
  TO: Company Security, Mr. B.A. Torenvliet

Number of pages:

3/22/9

Dear Mr. Torenvliet:

I just finished reading the letter from Commissaris Mollema which you se
to my attention. I am glad our own police has acted in this manner. Until
now I have not fully realized the dangers involved and I fully approve thei
initiative. I will personally contact Ackerman & Palumbo, Inc. and will tell
them that we do not appreciate the behavior of their operative. I have the
greatest possible confidence in the police forces supplied by Rotterdam
and The Hague and would prefer to let them decide strategy.

Sincerely,

Jm. Voute

J.M. Voute

RADICAL PEOPLE'S FRONT FOR AFRICA

number of pages: 1   to: Mr. Voute, Shell Netherlands

22 March 1990

!!!! FREEDOM FOR BLACK AFRICA !!!!

That was really dumb! But we were ready for it. It was really difficult for us to believe that a multinational would pay such an amount (although to them it is no more than Petty Cash) for the betterment of mankind. But we had thought that you would be more intelligent. You should have known that we would take precautions to check if the driver was being followed, or was passing some other kind of messages. We too, are aware of modern electronics and we know where we can buy the necessary equipment. How could you so underestimate us! How many volumes of Playboy did it take to fill the suitcase? Or is it possible that in your smug overestimation of yourself you did not even bother to carry a suitcase?

The chances we have offered you have not been used and we will draw our conclusions accordingly.

Phase 3 will now start and you will not easily forget what that means to you. We advise you to have the required amount in readiness <u>and</u> according to the demanded specifications for the different denominations. No more fairy tales about an "adjustment" in the correct coinage. There is less time left than you think! A hint: less than 3 days! You will not hear from us for a while, but I can assure you that when you <u>do</u> hear from us, you will remember it for a long time to come!

!!!! MANDELA IS FREE AND AFRICA WILL FOLLOW !!!!

---

aan/to	naam/name	t.a.v./attn.
X3864X2X367	The Hague Police	Comm. Vaart

---

van/from	naam/name	ref. no.
X2X35X86968	Shell	Torenvliet

---

aantal pag./number of pages: 4

The Hague, March 22, 199

Dear Mr. Vaart:

Herewith a copy of this morning's fax. The text is self-explanatory. It is now just a threatening letter. We did expect that. I still cannot understand that we have no leads at all. This case is my sole preoccupation, day and night. What are we missing? What do we have?

It can be assumed that a number of faxes were sent from abroad during the early stages. Time of transmission was always after 6PM and the response to ads in the Telegraaf was always a day later. We are asked to support the freedom fighters in Africa. The tone fluctuates between friendly and threatening. The impression is given that we are dealing with an organization consisting of several persons. We do not know how many. The organization is unknown and has never been heard of before. Amsterdam has been able to check that thoroughly.

This could mean that we are dealing with a new group, but it can also mean that we are dealing with a very small organization. The ideal for which they claim to fight, has become moot. Everybody knows that President de Klerk, slowly but surely, is in the process of doing away with apartheid. The process will take time, but a start has been made. This leads us to the theory that we are dealing with a farce. In other words, the motivation is money, pure and simple. But why this round-about way?

Do they really expect a concern like Shell to respond to their sentimental and idealistic arguments? Everything points to the fact that they are not dumb and that they possess information that has surprised us. Are they then not intelligent enough to realize that an organization like Shell will have information regarding political changes in Africa? Government

...aders all over the world, including South Africa, keep in close contact with Business & Industry. In the upper management circles of many companies more is known regarding political thoughts in the various countries than is readily available to the public. How can they be so dumb is not to include this in their calculations? Again, why this round-about way?

is just a stay of execution, for them, as well as for us. In the process they have wasted their own best weapon, that of surprise. They have warned and alerted us. This must make it more difficult for them to execute their plans. The only answer I can come up with is, that our opponent is so certain of success that he just wants to see us struggle. He is baiting us. so, in addition to money, we may be dealing with rancor, or revenge. against certain people, or perhaps against the entire firm.

One conclusion: A spiteful man with a superiority complex.

hen the murder of Hutters has to be taken into account. Although we have not found any conclusive proof, we may assume that he had some connection with the Front. The identical sentence structure in the "Hutters" ax and the Front fax from the next day, point in that direction. The method used to kill Hutters gives us a few additional "leads." It was a settling of accounts. The car had been prepared months in advance for just such a urpose, either for Hutters, or for somebody else. The person who prepared the car must have knowledge of explosives. More important, he must have known about detonators and specific detonation equipment. Therefore the person must have more than the usual knowledge of technical matters. He must also be aware of available supplies. Where is his type of information readily available? In the Near- and Far East and with terrorist organizations such as the IRA, the PLO and the ETA in Spain. If our theory, that the first faxes were transmitted from abroad, proves to be correct, he could have been in one of those countries at the time.

Conclusion: A man with a technical background who regularly stays abroad. Add to this: revenge and/or rancor against a person or persons unknown within the company, or against the entire company and self-assured of his own capabilities.

The failed action of yesterday again points to a technical background. The way in which the transmitter had been hidden behind the dashboard indicates experience. From the various technical tricks he uses, it is obvious that he has planned all the necessary possibilities to enable him to manipulate events from a distance. It is most certainly a small group. At most four people. The complete silence within the Amsterdam environment is another indication in that direction.

What next? All leads have led to a dead end. The origin of the faxes cannot be traced. There has been no voice contact. There is no leak within the firm. In any case, there is no proof that there is a leak. The tennis score of 6-4, 6-3 which was mentioned and which coincides with Mr. Voute's tennis score could have been coincidence. The South-American trip of Mr. Voute has been discussed in the Company Magazine. Hundreds of these are available, every month, in all our offices and plants.

What are we missing?

I will send a copy of this letter to Commissaris Mollema, Commissaris Bakkenist and to Mr. Voute.

Sincerely,

B.A. Torenvliet

AMSTERDAM MUNICIPAL POLICE

Headquarters: Marnixstraat

FAX TO:	ATTN:	NUMBER:	PAG.
Shell Security	Torenvliet	▚▚▚▚▚▚▚▚	1

----

22 March, 1990

Anton:

We checked along the Prince's Canal here in Amsterdam from where the red Ford Escort has been stolen. No results. As I expected, frankly. Just before sending this fax, I received your detailed letter recapitulating the entire affair. I cannot offer any suggestions as to where to look at this time. That there is any connection with Africa, is something I have not believed for some time. They are common criminals, out for money. It is too well planned and too well prepared to have been done by a single person. The reason for the soft-sell, the "humane" approach, may have been a red herring. For instance, because of this red herring we started to look in the wrong direction. We started to look among idealistic groups. There are so many organization that, one way or the other, want to save mankind. We know most of them. But with a few exceptions, there are no real criminals among them. That was known. Therefore we were on purpose sent up the garden path. Of course, they have given up the element of surprise, but in their eyes they gained because we were less alert, thinking we were dealing with a totally different kind of organization. In addition, they had the chance, however unlikely, that Shell would accede to their demands. Don't forget the argument that was used about "undue publicity". For some firms that would be a real concern. Some would rather have paid, then be held up to ridicule. Perhaps that is the answer to your question. These possibilities will be included in all roll-calls tomorrow and extra vigilance will be urged on all officers.

Greetings,

H. Bakkenist

Henk Bakkenist

RADICAL PEOPLE'S FRONT FOR AFRICA

number of pages: 1   to: Mr. Voute, Shell Netherlands

26 March 1990

!!!! FREEDOM FOR BLACK AFRICA !!!!

Today the day has come that you will beg us to pay! Just call the number ████████████████, which should be well known to you. Nobody will answer the phone. The man in question is now in our hands. The more radical elements in our organization, against whom I have warned you time and time again, have now taken control and you have nobody to blame but yourself. The hostage is in good health and will be treated as well as possible. Nobody knows better than you, however, that there is a severe time limit. We therefore advise you to settle this matter as soon as possible. Tonight at 23:00 you will receive a fax with a telephone number. You may send your answer within the usual 10 seconds.

---

aan/to	naam/name	t.a.v./attn.
X3864X2X367	The Hague Police	Comm. Vaart

---

van/from	naam/name	ref. no.
X2X35X0X68	Shell	Torenvliet

---

aantal pag./number of pages: 2

The Hague, March 26, 1990

Dear Mr. Vaart:

Herewith the fax about which I called you earlier. Also additional information about Ron Voute. He suffers from glomerulonephritis. The disease manifests itself as kidney poisoning in the most severe form. In order to be treated with dialysis he reports to the Academic Hospital three times per week. He usually checks in around 11PM and then spends the night there. He went last night and left this morning at 8:30 AM. The time limit mentioned in the fax from the Front is based on the absolute necessity for him to report back to the hospital no later than this coming Wednesday night. Delay of treatment will be fatal.

I don't have to emphasize the need for speed in this particular case. We have instructed our bank to assemble the required amounts and have it delivered to us no later than 3PM today.

When you receive this fax, I will already be en-route to you.

Anton Torenvliet

B.A. Torenvliet

CC: Rotterdam
    Amsterdam

FROM: Administration of Mr. J.M. Voute
  TO: ALL DEPARTMENTS

Number of pages: 1

3/26/90

TO WHOM IT MAY CONCERN:

EFFECTIVE IMMEDIATELY: BECAUSE OF THE SERIOUS SITUATION
CREATED BY THE KIDNAPPING OF HIS SON AS A HOSTAGE, ALL
FUNCTIONS OF MR. VOUTE WILL BE HANDLED BY DR. W.W. STORK
UNTIL FURTHER NOTICE.

UNDER NO CIRCUMSTANCES IS ANY INFORMATION TO BE GIVEN
TO THE PRESS, REGARDING THIS MATTER, OR ANY OTHER
MATTER.

MANAGEMENT.

EASTERN ORGAN BANK, Inc.

TO: Dr. E. Branger
    Leiden Academic Hospital
    NETHERLANDS

3-26-90

Dear Dr. Branger:

Last night we received one kidney, suitable for your patient, R. Voute. ETA will be 7:30 AM (local time) via PanAm Flight 389.

The accompanying technical assistant is Mrs. J.P. Adams, MD.

Sincerely,

Dr. A.M. Ashton

ROYAL DUTCH SHELL
SHELL NEDERLAND

Headquarters Administration   *   **Hofplein**   *   **Rotterdam**

FACSIMILE MESSAGE TO: Municipal Police Amsterdam,
                                      Rotterdam & The Hague
             ATTN: Commissaris Bakkenist   NR OF PAG: 1
                      Commissaris Mollema
                      Commissaris Vaart

Rotterdam, 19 February, 1990

Dear Sirs:

On behalf of Shell Management and Mr. Voute I want to make the
following request: Please take no action which will endanger the life of the
hostage, Ron Voute.

As you know, Mr. Voute, Jr. suffers from a serious kidney disease. It is of
the utmost importance that this hostage crisis be resolved within the
shortest possible time, because the patient <u>must</u> have medical attention
within two days.

We will acquiesce to any demand for payment.

Sincerely,

W. m Stork

Dr. W.W. Stork

THE HAGUE MUNICIPAL POLICE

Headquarters: Peace Palace Straat

FAX TO: **ATTN:**   **NUMBER:**   **PAG.**
                  ALL POINTS BULLETIN!
_____

26 March, 1990

Dear Colleagues:

In connection with the kidnapping of Ron Voute, son of the Managing Director of Shell/Nederland, herewith the following:

We have, for the fourth time, received a fax wherein we were told to expect a specific phone number at 23:00 tonight.

We have been instructed to respond (by fax) within 10 seconds after receipt of the fax.

We know from experience that we will be transmitting to a small firm in an isolated area. Usually at least 15 km. from the nearest police station.

I urgently request that you utilize as many personnel as possible to give extra attention to likely places within your jurisdiction.

We do not know the type of car being used, but it is assumed that the suspect will try to leave the area in haste, between 23:01 and 23:05.

Thank You.

A. W. Vaart

Commissaris A.W. Vaart
         ALL POINTS BULLETIN!

RADICAL PEOPLE'S FRONT FOR AFRICA

number of pages: 1   to: Mr. Voute, Shell Netherlands

!!!! FREEDOM FOR BLACK AFRICA !!!!

RPFA:

The money, according to your exact specifications, is ready. We want to pay! Tell us what to do. We solemnly promise that no police will be involved. Delivery will be made by Dr. W.W. Stork, Assistant Managing Director of our firm. He will be driving a grey BMW with license tag # BA-48-XS. He will be unarmed and will have no transmitters, or any other kind of communication equipment.

You win!

RADICAL PEOPLE'S FRONT FOR AFRICA

number of pages: 1   to: Mr. Voute, Shell Netherlands

27 March 1990

!!!! FREEDOM FOR BLACK AFRICA !!!!

A small difficulty has come up. I have told you that certain elements within our organization are more radical than your correspondent. Your foolish actions of yesterday have created unrest and voices are being raised to increase the amount to $10 million. After heated debate we voted democratically for a unanimous proposal. Mostly through my efforts and because of my empathy for the hostage, I have been able to persuade our committee to increase the price by just one million ($1,000,000). This was considered reasonable under the circumstances. The extra money should be in US dollars. We feel you owe us some compensation for the difficulties created by your foolish actions.

I am able to tell you that the hostage is still in good health.

You will be contacted at 23:00

THE HAGUE MUNICIPAL POLICE

Headquarters: Peace Palace Straat

FAX TO:	ATTN:	NUMBER:	PAG.
Shell Security	Torenvliet	███████████	2

27 March, 1990

Dear Mr. Torenvliet:

The number we received from the Front belonged to a car phone. It was a Mercedes, license number VD-89-RS, belonging to Mr. W.F. van Maanen of 30 Tromp Lane in Edam. We visited Mr. Van Maanen that same night and it was then discovered that the car had disappeared. He said he came home around 7PM that night and, as usual, had parked his car in the street. We have sent a telex to all police stations, but the car has not yet been found.

The Phone Company provided the following technical details. The perpetrator must have a battery-operated fax machine. It is a relatively simple procedure to connect this to a car phone. Sometimes this feature is built into the car phone, but even if that is not the case, it takes less than a few minutes to complete the (temporary) installation. A fax can then be used. That means, of course, that the suspect can be anywhere in the Netherlands (or Belgium). It is even possible that he received our fax while driving.

The theft of the car would, under normal circumstances, not have been discovered until the next morning, because Mr. Van Maanen has a pretty regular schedule. The question is whether the perpetrator knows Mr. Van Maanen, or whether he has been following him for some time. Another possibility is that he has stolen a likely car with a car phone. The extra antenna clearly identifies such a car. All in all a very shrewd (and new) way to lead us by the nose.

I have also consulted with my colleagues in Amsterdam and Rotterdam and want to ask you, also on their behalf, to discuss the following with Messrs Stork and Voute:

We will stay away from the delivery of the money. At the time that the exchange place is known, we will inform the local police and request that all patrol cars be re-called in order to prevent one of them passing the location by accident, which could be fatal to the quick exchange of money and information. We would appreciate it, however, if you will understand that we want to place some people at about 200 meters from the rendez-vous in order to record license tags of vehicles moving in and out of the area. That will be our only activity at the time. We will not take any other steps until after we have been informed that Mr. Voute's son has been found.

Sincerely,

A.W. Vaart

Commissaris A.W. Vaart

ROYAL DUTCH SHELL
SHELL NEDERLAND

Headquarters Administration   *   Hofplein   *   Rotterdam

FACSIMILE MESSAGE TO: Restaurant Tristan
ATTN: Mr. Torenvliet

NR OF PAG: 1

Rotterdam, 27 March, 1990

Dear Mr. Torenvliet:

Mr. Voute and I discussed the proposal made by Commissaris Vaart and
we completely agree with the proposed actions of the police. Mr. Voute
has full confidence in the professionalism and restraint of the police and
expresses the hope that this will help to effect a speedy arrest.

Sincerely,

W.W. Stork
Acting Managing Director

TO MRS. CARLA VINK

Rotterdam, 27 March, 1990

Dear Carla:

You will not receive today's paper until tomorrow, therefore I'll drop you a quick note. Yesterday morning they kidnapped Mr. Voute's son and they are keeping him as a hostage. It is horrible. He had apparently just left the Academic Hospital where he has to go three times per week for dialysis. We had been expecting something awful because of all these threatening letters we have been receiving over the fax. Anybody of any importance had extra security assigned and Mr. Voute had even somebody in his house on a permanent basis. But nobody could have suspected that they would take it out on the son. Everything points to the fact that the kidnappers are fully aware of Ron's disability. You cannot help but wonder what type of people would do such a thing. It is a madhouse around here. As far as I know, the police have no leads. Last week a meeting with the same group fell completely apart. In retrospect, they would have been better off just to give them the damn money, that way poor Ron would now still be able to get treatment. As you can tell, things are in an uproar around here.

I don't know anything else to write at the moment, but this seems enough.

Love,

Janny

RADICAL PEOPLE'S FRONT FOR AFRICA

number of pages: 1   to: Mr. Voute, Shell Netherlands

27 March 1990

!!!! FREEDOM FOR BLACK AFRICA !!!!

Depart immediately after receiving this fax in the direction of Amsterdam. Follow main road to Utrecht. After about 3 km take the exit toward Aalsmeer. At the traffic circle turn left toward the Ring Canal. Follow that road until you reach the second viaduct. Stop at the right side of the road, under the viaduct and place the money in a closed, black plastic bag against the pillar marked with a white x. Then disappear. Two hours after the delivery of the money we will send you a fax with the address at which your son can be found. If the police takes any steps within this two hour limit, or if there is anything wrong with the money, you will never see your son again. If the police tries to stop the delivery, they should realize that they can at most just catch <u>one</u> person of our organization.

Leave now.

THE HAGUE MUNICIPAL POLICE

Headquarters: Peace Palace Straat

FAX TO:	**ATTN:**	**NUMBER:**	**PAG.**
Shell Security	Torenvliet	✖✖✖✖✖✖✖✖✖✖✖✖✖✖	4

28 March, 1990

Dear Mr. Torenvliet:

Herewith a synopsis of the events of last night and the first results of our investigations. Mr. Stork, driving his own BMW, arrived at the place of delivery at 00:23. As agreed, we had placed people at 200 meter distance in both directions from the place indicated. The fact that the road ran along a canal facilitated covering the area. We used nondescript cars and vans. Our people noted the license tags and descriptions of all vehicles passing on the road itself, as well as on the road running across the top of the viaduct. This proved to be pointless.

We saw Mr. Stork get out of the car with the bag containing the $6 million and we saw him place the bag against the marked pillar. At that moment a car approached and stopped. A heated discussion developed between the driver of the other car and Mr. Stork. Apparently the passing motorist was under the impression that Mr. Stork was getting rid of his garbage. Mr. Stork did get back in his car and both cars drove off.

We waited for two hours. Nothing happened during that time. Cars passed but nobody stopped. It was a very dark night without moon and heavily overcast, which impaired vision. We maintained continuous contact with your Main Office in order to get immediate word regarding the fax from the Front with the address of Ron Voute. I assume that this has not yet been received. I am convinced that it will not come. After consulting with your people, we took action at 3:30 AM and approached the place where the bag had been left.

We found that the bag had disappeared. Certain that no car had stopped and also certain that nothing else had happened, we started our investigations at that time and place. About 45 meters from the spot we found a small house boat. The local police informed us that this was generally only used on summer week-ends and had not been used at all, for some months. In front of the house boat we found fresh tire marks and the imprints of rubber boots. We searched the outside of the boat and obtained permission from the local police to force the door. We found the boat had two spaces, a bedroom and a living room. The bedroom was almost empty and we found that a hole had been made in the side away from the shore, just above the water line. In the other room we found the remains of Ron Voute on a bench, covered with some blankets.

Preliminary investigations showed that the victim had been dead for at least 36 hours. Shortly after having been transported to the houseboat he must have been killed with a single shot through the head. The murder weapon was a .38 revolver equipped with silencer. Immediately upon discovery of the body, the full resources of Amsterdam, Rotterdam and our own offices have been mobilized.

Here are the preliminary results:

On the roof of the houseboat we found a semi-professional, highly light-sensitive TV camera connected to a TV monitor in the living space of the houseboat. The suspect must have been able to follow all events under the viaduct. A sickening detail is that one of our people, about fifteen minutes before Mr. Stork's arrival, noticed a man watching television. The fact that he did not even bother to close the curtains, gives some indication of his smug complacency.

The money disappeared this way: When the suspect felt that the time was right and after having observed on his screen that the coast was clear, he donned a black scuba suit, went into the water through the hole in the hull and swam underwater to the spot under the viaduct. His street clothes were found in the house boat and traces of a black wetsuit were found on the edges of the hole. The distance between the water's edge and the plastic bag was 3.75 meters, or about 14 feet. As noted, it was an unusually dark night, no moon and overcast. In addition an extra shadow was created by the viaduct and the suspect was dressed in black. It was a relatively simple matter, under these circumstances, to recover a black bag. The damage to the vegetation at the water's edge seem to confirm this scenario.

After this the perpetrator must have swam underwater for some distance, to a place where a vehicle, or other means of transportation had been placed in advance. We're are still in the process of looking for the spot where he may have landed. We are also conducting a house-to-house search in the immediate neighborhood. All experts are still either at the scene, or available, for further investigations.

It is now certain that the entire operation has been planned and executed by a very small group. The brain behind it all is cunning and astute and has a disturbing amount of intimate knowledge about Shell's Management and the direct environment of the various management personnel. Your theory that the man may have been abroad, could be true, but that must have been a temporary situation. Another reason to keep looking within our immediate circle.

Hutters was no more than temporary help, to cover the period he had to be absent, but while it was necessary to continue operations. Hutters was also his source of information. He had to be kept informed regarding certain developments. But how could Hutters get the necessary information? When Hutters became superfluous, or perhaps an inconvenience, he was removed. The Toyota was prepared for just such a job. The motive is money, no more no less.

I will complete some ongoing matters today and then will be able to concentrate full-time on this case. Rotterdam and Amsterdam have promised the cooperation of special task forces.

Sincerely,

A.W. Vaart

Commissaris A.W. Vaart

ACADEMIC HOSPITAL
LEIDEN

DATE: 3/28/90
TO: Professor P.M. Vos
Academic Hospital Utrecht
FROM: Dr. J.D. Booy
REF: Kidney

Leiden, March 28, 1990

Dear Colleague:

We just received a kidney from the Eastern Organ Bank in Boston. The computer matches blood group and HLA tests with the next recipient in line, your patient Mrs. T. Van Loonen, born 4/23/61 in Arnhem. You should start your preparations. You can expect us around 13:00 today.

Sincerely,

J D de Booy

J.D. Booy, MD

THE HAGUE MUNICIPAL POLICE

Headquarters: Peace Palace Straat

AX TO:	ATTN:	NUMBER:	PAG.
hell Security	Torenvliet	████████████	2

28 March, 1990

Dear Mr. Torenvliet:

Mrs. Hutters called me half an hour ago. She told me she had found a pair of work pants belonging to her husband. Before throwing them away, as is her habit, she checked the pockets. In one of the pockets she found a fax, which she just delivered. Herewith the copy:

****

Received information. Thanks. Phase 2 will now start.

Check again and make sure all notes and faxes have been destroyed. There must not be any notes, or whatever, left. We cannot be too careful.

At 8 o'clock tonight proceed to the Bayberry Street in Voorburg. There is three-story apartment building, starting with number 36. There is a row of garages behind this building. The key, which you received from me at the time, will fit on the door of garage Number 4. Make sure you are not seen and that the parking area is empty before approaching the garage. Wait, if necessary. In the garage you will find a bronze Toyota. You will find the keys on top of the right front tire. Take the car to Schiphol Airport and park in Lot Number P3, as close as possible to Slot F2. Leave the parking ticket in the car.

It is hereby proved that Hutters killing was murder and was premeditated. Also his connection with the Front is certain. The letter type is identical with that on the faxes received from you. Although he does not mention the organization by name, he betrayed himself in the text. He mentioned "Phase 2". In the fax of March 22 he said "Phase 3 will now start". It is now absolutely certain that Hutters was his accomplice.

Mrs. Hutters is currently talking to two detectives in order to obtain a list of friends and relations. We must concentrate in that direction. It is our only solid lead.

Regarding ongoing investigations: The tire marks found near the house boat are identical with those found near the firm in Zuiderveld, where the first break-in occurred. Additionally, after a thorough search a .38 Smith & Wesson with silencer was found in the canal near the houseboat. Although we are almost certain that this is the murder weapon, we are conducting tests. The weapon was not registered.

Sincerely,

A. W. Vaart

Commissaris A.W. Vaart

ATTENTION: Mrs. J.A. Sijtsma
Headquarters Administration

BRUNEI, March 28, 1990

Dear Janny:

I just heard everything on the World Broadcast. How terrible! It is really horrible that children can become the victim, just because their parents have an important position. Everybody in the compound talks about it with disgust. Could one of our own people have done it? It is difficult to imagine. One must be a thoroughly bad person to be able to kill such a defenseless boy. I feel sorry for the family. I cannot stop thinking about it. It makes you feel so helpless.

Don't let it affect you too much, though, that it not good in your condition.

Love from all of us,

Carla

THE HAGUE MUNICIPAL POLICE

Headquarters: Peace Palace Straat

FAX TO:	**ATTN:**	**NUMBER:**	**PAG.**
Shell Security	Torenvliet	░░░░░░░░░░	2

28 March, 1990

Dear Mr. Torenvliet:

Herewith a list of employees with your firm who belong (i.e. belonged) to the circle of friends and relations of the Hutters family. It will be necessary to check the alibis of all of them and to check their background as well. I would like to request from you information about their service records and other, important data, such as travels, assignments abroad, mentality, etc.

The fax supplied by Mrs. Hutters has been carefully compared with the Front faxes. The letter type is identical, as I expected.

Sincerely,

a. W. Vaart

Commissaris A.W. Vaart

TO: Mr. B.A. Torenvliet / Security
FROM: Jules Hafkamp
REF:
PAGES: 1
DATE: 3/28/90

ear Anton:

he press release we published this morning, has, of course, elicited a
umber of reactions. I have been able to keep the press in check for now,
ut it is only a matter of time. I suggest we discuss the limits on the
mount of information to be released. If possible, I would like to include the
olice in our discussions. I will remain in the office, waiting for a speedy
ply.

reetings,

Jules Hafkamp

ules Hafkamp

THE HAGUE MUNICIPAL POLICE

Headquarters: Peace Palace Straat

FAX TO:	ATTN:	NUMBER:	PAG.
Shell PR	Mr. Hafkamp	▮▮▮▮▮▮▮▮▮▮▮	1

28 March, 199

Dear Mr. Hafkamp:

I have been forwarded your fax to Mr. Torenvliet. You hereby have permission to release the facts, as contained in my messages to Mr. Torenvliet, to the press. Just one restriction, in order to aid in the solution of this case: Although we are now almost certain that we are looking for a single person, I would like to request that you not reveal this to the press. Talk about an organization, the Radical People's Front for Africa. Create the impression we are sure to be dealing with this organization and that we are convinced it is a relatively large group, led by a person in the near East. Lebanon, Libya, or something like that. You may also want to mention that the serial numbers of all money has been registered and conveyed to all important banks around the world.

If necessary, you may refer the press to me.

With best wishes,

A. W. Vaart

Commissaris A.W. Vaart

THE HAGUE MUNICIPAL POLICE

Headquarters: Peace Palace Straat

FAX TO:	ATTN:	NUMBER:	PAG.
Shell Security	Torenvliet	▓▓▓▓▓▓▓▓▓▓	1

29 March, 1990

Dear Mr. Torenvliet:

During the investigations of Hutters' friends and
relations we found a very important connection. This
information must be restricted for your eyes only. I therefore
request that you be alone in the fax room when I transmit
this to you. Please call when you are ready to receive.

P.W. Vaart

Commissaris A.W. Vaart

THE HAGUE MUNICIPAL POLICE

Headquarters: Peace Palace Straat

FAX TO:	ATTN:	NUMBER:	PAG.
Shell Security	Torenvliet	████████████	3

29 March, 1990

Dear Mr. Torenvliet:

Upon checking the background of Mr. W.W. Stork, Acting Managing Director, residing at Nassau Lane 14, Voorburg, we made a number of disturbing discoveries. Mr. Stork speculates heavily and on margin, according to reports received from the Amro Bank. His speculations include stocks, options, futures markets and foreign exchange markets. He has lost an amount in excess of f359,000 on his transactions as of December 31 of last year. On the 8th of January the Bank requested him to make a deposit of f350,000 to offset margin calls and as additional security regarding ongoing obligations. On March 5 of this year he suffered an additional loss of f361,500 in margin calls. Again the Bank requested additional margin and sureties. Until last year he carried a first and a second mortgage to a value of f650,000 on his house in Voorburg. After his latest loss on March 5, he managed to obtain a third mortgage at 14% from a bank in Belgium. We do not yet have a complete breakdown of all his obligations, but it seems that Mr. Stork is heavily over extended and may well be in serious financial trouble. He recently closed a futures contract which obligates him to buy $1,500,000 US dollars at a price of f1.90. Theoretically Mr. Stork is bankrupt, according to financial experts at Amro Bank, unless he can dispose of additional, unlisted capital. There is no information regarding additional sources of income.

This could be a motive and he would make an ideal suspect, especially in light of a number of coincidences. I wish to point to certain information, known to, or supplied by, the Front which could only be known to intimate acquaintances of Mr. Voute, to wit:

) Score of tennis match at The Hall
) Details of South-American trip
) Stay in hotels and dates
) Type of illness suffered by R. Voute
) Days that R. Voute attended hospital
) Second house in France

Twice Mr. Stork volunteered to make contact with the kidnappers, an action not devoid of a certain amount of risk! Especially not in the case of the suitcase filled with worthless paper. If, however, he is indeed the brain behind the organization, he had nothing to fear! Perhaps that's why he volunteered. After the second "meeting" the money disappeared. A very slick way to make it disappear. But we should take into consideration that the placing of the bag with money, by Mr. Stork, facilitated the recovery by the diver. We were instructed to place the bag near the marked pillar. The bag could have been placed on the road-side of the pillar, or on the water-side. If the bag had been placed on the road-side, the diver would have had more trouble to remove it unseen. But the bag was placed on the water-side of the pillar. This could have been coincidence, but you and I don't believe in coincidences.

I have assigned two detectives to Mr. Stork and they will do a complete and thorough background check. I will also call him in for an interrogation and I will discuss the matter with the Judge-Advocate. We may have enough facts to obtain a Search Warrant.

Please gather all available information about Mr. Stor[
and contact me at your earliest possible opportunity.

Sincerely,

A.W. Vaart

Commissaris A.W. Vaart

Rotterdam, 30 March, 1990

ear Carla:

Quickly a short note. Nothing but bad news, I'm afraid. Yvonne averman has attempted suicide. Leni, the cleaning lady, found her this orning. She had taken an overdose of sleeping pills but, thank God, t enough. She has been transported to the hospital and is still in a ma. I am totally confused and very upset. It seems we are faced with e terrible incident after another. First the murder of Henk Hutters, then r. Voute's son and now this. I cannot understand it. I talked to her almost ily and she seemed to have everything under control. She was so happy out the renewed contact with her sister and that she would be living th her from now on. I always cheered up after talking to her. She was ways so happy! I don't mind admitting that it is all getting to be a little o much for me. It is a madhouse here. All day long I run from my office the fax room, because the fax doesn't seem to stop. Police, Torenvliet Security, Stork, you name it. Everybody is sending, receiving, following , starting up and nobody knows what the others are doing.

The office is on a 24-hour shift and police are present in all departments. st night I went home around 5 in order to get some rest and at 7 that me night I had to be back again. Finally got home after midnight and as back again before nine. And now, just half an hour ago, this news out Yvonne. I expect Mr. Stork any moment. He was here until after ree this morning. But as soon as he comes in, I'll ask him for permission pack it in for the rest of the day. There are enough young girls around ere who are not as close to the various victims and are less personally uched by it all. I have to get away from it all. I want to go to the hospital d I want to be there when Yvonne recovers from her coma. I am sure e can use my help. I'll be more use there. Mr. Voute is at home and as withdrawn from everything. I really feel sorry for those two old people.

I take it you have received yesterday's papers where there is a complete port as to how the crooks managed the affair. The money is gone and e suspects have also disappeared.

ove,

Janny

THE HAGUE MUNICIPAL POLICE

Headquarters: Peace Palace Straat

FAX TO:	ATTN:	NUMBER:	PAG.
Shell Security	Torenvliet	███████████	1

30 March, 199

Dear Mr. Torenvliet:

As a result of the suicide attempt of Mrs. Staverman, we
have started an investigation of her husband's past. Apparently he used to be employed by your firm and seems to have
been stationed in Brunei for the last five years. The couple
returned to Holland on March 12, after a stay of five years i
Brunei. Although the husband seemed pretty upset as a
result of his wife's suicide attempt, he was willing to talk to
us. He started on March 14 as Manager of the Technical
Department of a large retail chain. We contacted the firm an
the information checks. We received a list of the branches h
has visited during the last few weeks and we contacted the
various store managers. He has indeed visited the various
branches on the days specified. On the day of the kidnapping
and murder he was apparently at home, which could have
been confirmed by his wife, were she not in a coma. As far a
I can see, we are here dealing with a true coincidence, not
connected to the current case. From a different source I
learned that she has previously been counseled by a
psychiatrist for severe depression and tendency to suicide.
Another reason to assume that this case is not connected
with the Voute case. Nevertheless, I would appreciate some
additional information about this ex-employee.

Sincerely,

A.W. Vaart

Commissaris A.W. Vaart

R. J.K. GOUDSWAARD
R. F.W. GOUDSWAARD
R. R.E.K. BENCKHUYZEN
RS. B. DE RIDDER-MICHAELSEN

TTORNEYS-AT-LAW
RINSES ANNA LAAN 11
509 XT DEN HAAG

HONE: ~~XX82938X82~~
AX: ~~8X382X582938~~

AX MESSAGE FOR COMMISSARIS VAART
THE HAGUE MUNICIPAL POLICE

30 March, 1990

ear Mr Vaart:

rs. Sijtsma informed me this morning about the suicide attempt of Mrs.
averman. Mrs. Sijtsma knows that I represent Mrs. Staverman and her
ounger sister, Bianca van de Brink, in a suit against their father, G.J. van
e Brink, born 12-11-46 at Gouda. Mr. van de Brink currently lives in Delft
nd is accused of incest. The report has been filed with the police in
aasland on March 14, 1990. Because the younger sister had to be
moved from the parental home, Juvenile Protection has placed her in
e care of her older sister. Because of all this I have, during the last few
eeks, been in close contact with Mrs. Staverman. The news of her
uicide attempt surprised me, because it is in direct contradiction to the
ay I perceived Mrs. Staverman since her return to Holland. There simply
as no indication that she would contemplate such a thing. On the
ontrary, her demeanor and attitude have been consistently optimistic and
ositive. The fact that she volunteered to be responsible for her younger
ster is some sort of indication of her attitude. Perhaps you are aware of
er past, unpleasant history. But this recent act of desperation does not
onform to her current attitude to life and her surroundings. There is no
ay to make me believe that she would have attempted suicide under the
esent circumstances.

herefore, I would urge you to carefully investigate this apparent suicide

221

and not to be solely guided by information about her past, which can only serve to distract you from the true nature of the case. It is known that she has been threatened several times by her father, even after her marriage. In view of the current situation, I wanted to make sure that you were aware of this part of the pre-history.

I will be available for further information, if required.

Sincerely,

B. de Ridder-Michaelsen, Esquire

---

an/to	naam/name	t.a.v./attn.
~~3864828367~~	The Hague Police	Comm. Vaart

---

an/from	naam/name	ref. no.
~~2435450963~~	Shell	Torenvliet

---

antal pag./number of pages: 1

The Hague, March 30, 1990

ear Mr. Vaart:

ereby the information you requested:

driaan Johan Staverman
orn: 12 March, 1956 at Schoorl
larried to Yvonne Antoinette van de Brink
orn: 23 February, 1968 at Rotterdam

service from May 15, 1981 through March 10, 1990
rofession: Electronic Technician

ood service record. Little contact with colleagues. Somewhat of a loner,
artly because of nature of duties. Separation was voluntary. No important
etails are known about the time spent in Brunei. Local management was
xtremely satisfied with his performance.

ast leave in Holland during August, 1989

Anton Torenvliet

Anton Torenvliet]

.A. Torenvliet

THE HAGUE MUNICIPAL POLICE

Headquarters: Peace Palace Straat

FAX TO:	ATTN:	NUMBER:	PAG.
Shell Security	Torenvliet	▓▓▓▓▓▓▓▓▓▓	3

30 March, 199

Dear Mr. Torenvliet:

Herewith a fax just received from Mrs. de Ridder, Esquire. On the basis of this report I have decided to re-open the investigation regarding the attempted suicide of Mrs. Staverman. Please send me a photo of Staverman by messenger. Is the correspondence between Mrs. Vink and Mrs. Sijtsma still available?

Sincerely,

a. W. Vaart

Commissaris A.W. Vaart

ROYAL DUTCH SHELL
SHELL NEDERLAND

Headquarters Administration   *   Hofplein   *   Rotterdam

FACSIMILE MESSAGE TO: The Hague Municipal Police
ATTN: Comm. Vaart   NR OF PAG: 17

Rotterdam, 30 March, 1990

Dear Mr. Vaart:

At the request of Mr. Torenvliet I am forwarding to you copies of the correspondence between myself and Mrs. Vink during the last few months.

Hoping to have been of service, I remain,

Sincerely,

J Sytsma

Mrs. Sijtsma

THE HAGUE MUNICIPAL POLICE

Headquarters: Peace Palace Straat

FAX TO:	**ATTN:**	**NUMBER:**	**PAG.**
Maasland Fire Dept.	Mr. Oostrom	▚▚▚▚▚▚▚▚▚	1

30 March, 1990

Dear Mr. Oostrom:

During September of last year there was a fire at Number 18, Zandweg within your jurisdiction. A farm house was partially destroyed. This may be connected to a current investigation. Please forward a complete report regarding this particular fire.

Sincerely,

A.W. Vaart

Commissaris A.W. Vaart

THE HAGUE MUNICIPAL POLICE

Headquarters: Peace Palace Straat

FAX TO:	ATTN:	NUMBER:	PAG.
Shell Security	Torenvliet	████████████	2

31 March, 1990

Dear Mr. Torenvliet:

After further investigation, including medical evidence gathered by the police surgeon, it has been established that the suicide attempt of Mrs. Staverman, to say the least, is subject to review.

Because Mrs. Staverman filed a complaint against her father for incest, we did take into consideration the possibility of revenge on the part of the father. To that end he has been brought in for questioning. It seems unlikely, however, that he is connected to the Voute case.

I have also scheduled Mr. Stork for an interrogation. At this time we are checking his alibis. He is the only one with an acceptable motive at this time. The man is in a hopeless financial position, is extremely intelligent and completely aware of all events within the Company. If there is indeed a "brain" behind all of this, then Stork is the most likely candidate.

The question of his accomplices then remains to be solved. Because of the consummate attention to details we have encountered, I am almost sure that his alibis will be virtually untouchable. He is a man with the sort of self-confidence that strikes one as irritating and arrogant. I find it hard to believe that he committed the murders himself, or even planned them. Events may simply have overtaken him.

If we are forced, because of lack of evidence, to let him go, it will be almost impossible to track down the real killers. A frustrating thought.

I will keep you informed.

a. W. Vaart

Commissaris A.W. Vaart

MAASLAND FIRE DEPARTMENT
Kerkstraat 1 * Telefoon: XX2O4XX79З * Fax: 4XX72O4XX

March 31, 1990

Dear Mr. Vaart:

In response to your request I can report the following: We received a call concerning a fire at the Zandweg 18, around 20:33 hours on 29 September, 1989.

The fire was located in a farmhouse which had been remodelled as a single family residence. The house retained its original straw roof. When we arrived on the scene it was evident that the roof had caught fire and we immediately proceeded with the usual measures to control and extinguish the fire. Partly because of the prevailing weather conditions it did not take long to get the fire under control, but the back part of the house was lost to the flames.

Because we knew that the owners were not in residence and would be abroad for an extended period, we started a thorough investigation as to the causes of the fire. Arson was suspected.

After investigation this was ruled out. The fire was caused by an explosion precipitated by a leak in the gas supply to the house. The observations from neighbors confirmed this conclusion. During the investigation we found a number of timing devices, designed to switch lights on and off. One of these devices was slightly different from the others. In addition to daily time settings, this particular model was also capable of monthly settings. The remains were, however, so thoroughly destroyed as a result of the fire, that no evidence could be found to lead us to suspect other than an accidental fire, set off by a leak in the gas supply.

I do not know how this information can be of help to you in your current investigations, but one of my people is en-route to you with the complete report and the remains of the timing devices.

With friendly greetings,

W. Oostrom

THE HAGUE MUNICIPAL POLICE

Headquarters: Peace Palace Straat

FAX TO:	**ATTN:**	**NUMBER:**	**PAG.**
Shell Security	Brunei	XXXXXXXXXXXXX	1

31 March, 1990

TO WHOM IT MAY CONCERN:

In connection with an ongoing investigation regarding the kidnapping and murder of Mr. Ron Voute, son of your Managing Director, I would like to request all available information concerning Mr. Arie Staverman.

Mr. Staverman departed for Holland on March 12, 1990 after a 5-year tour of duty with your operation. All particulars concerning his stay in Brunei, especially during the last 12 months, are of the greatest importance and will aid in a rapid solution of the case. Please respond at your earliest opportunity.

Sincerely,

a.W. Vaart

Commissaris A.W. Vaart

SHELL BRUNEI

Compound Management

DATE: March 31, 1990

TO: Commissaris Vaart / The Hague Municipal Police
FROM: G.M. Van Der Ploeg / Chief Security, Shell-Brunei
REF: Your Fax of 3-31-90

Dear Mr. Vaart:

Herewith the initial response to your request.

Mr. Staverman was employed here as an Electronic Technician. He is an excellent craftsman and the management was extremely pleased with his performance. A very correct and conscientious worker, always aware of the smallest details. Yet, I should inform you that he was less than popular with his colleagues. Upon further information he was found to be extremely arrogant, full of his own importance and always conscious of his own capabilities, which he thought to be limitless. He also mentioned several times that he would be working for a "really large" concern upon his return to the Netherlands.

In October of last year, he started a friendship with a Libyan. Not an unusual occurrence in a compound where several nationalities all work for the same company. His friend, however, was arrested in December of that same year for the smuggling of weapons and drugs. We have contacted the local authorities but were unable to get any details. Not unusual in this country.

As you may know, houses for personnel are provided fully furnished and when a family leaves, the house is restored, repaired and/or refurnished as needed, to its original specifications before the next family moves in. There are as yet no new residents for the house vacated by the Stavermans and the house is still in the state as it was left upon their departure.

The houses are identical. Outlets, switches, appliances, phone connections, etc. are all located in the same places. Underneath all the houses, which are built on poles, a storage area has been installed. We noticed in the Staverman house that the phone line had been extended to within this storage space. Near the outlet, in the dust on an abandoned table, we found the outline of four legs, or feet, as used at the bottom of a fax machine, or printer, as used by many of our personnel.

Because we have been made aware that the search is for an organization that sent faxes from abroad, we felt the circumstances of this discovery rather suspicious. Why would anybody take so much trouble to move a fax machine? Apart from Mrs. Vink, who twice a week runs a sort of pre-kindergarten in a similar space, nobody has ever used this type of space for anything else than storage of unwanted, or unneeded items. Also the fact that a diver was used to recover the money from along the canal drew our attention. Staverman was an enthusiastic skin- and scuba diver.

You probably should also know that the family took extra emergency leave during the period October 1 through October 7, 1989 because of a fire at their Maasland residence in Holland. They went to Holland during that period in order to take care of insurance and other matters. Their regular annual leave was in August. Generally they spent that in Holland as well.

You are probably aware that Mrs. Staverman tried to commit suicide about two years ago. She was treated in the compound hospital and as far as is known, she has completely recovered from whatever it was that caused her to try suicide.

In case anything else surfaces, we will inform you at once.

With friendly greetings,

G.M. Van Der Ploeg

THE HAGUE MUNICIPAL POLICE

Headquarters: Peace Palace Straat

FAX TO:	ATTN:	NUMBER:	PAG.
Shell Security	Torenvliet	▚▛▞▞▚▜▚▞▚▜▞▞	14

31 March, 1990

Dear Mr. Torenvliet:

Yesterday we met a completely devastated Arie Staverman, because of the "suicide" attempt of his wife, Yvonne. How one can be mistaken! The paths chosen by the criminal brain, coupled with a high intelligence, are inscrutable and almost incapable of solution by the most modern police methods. Time and time again we find that, despite high-tech equipment and scientifically equipped laboratories, we cannot outguess the actions of a loner. Because it is now clear. The entire Radical People's Front for Africa and all subsequent events thereto were the work of just one man: Arie Staverman. To the last he remained out of sight and nobody gave him another thought. He never gave us any reason to look at him closer.

Your theory of March 22 describes him well: A self-satisfied, arrogant and spiteful man with a technical background, probably residing in the East. Not liked by colleagues. Very sure of own capabilities. A craftsman, detail oriented and precise. All characteristics that have shown themselves during the development of the case. In addition an enthusiastic underwater sportsman! As icing on the cake. Please refer to the copy of the fax (attachment 1) recently received from Brunei.

The man remained extremely cool under fire. Had immense self-control and had planned for every eventuality. The usual characteristics of a person used to think in

233

technical terms. We can be sure he even prepared for a "third degree". Because of the temporary job he accepted, he was able to produce a number of reasonable alibis which were easily checked against his travel logs. If that proved to be impossible, he would simply declare to have been at home. His wife would then be the only witness, but she, unfortunately, is in a coma. That is one of his few mistakes, because he fully intended to kill her.

Yesterday we discovered that he is not only a criminal genius, but also a gifted actor. His sorrow was so real, that nobody suspected any different. But she was the only one left able to testify against him. Therefore he staged her suicide. Upon further investigation we asked if it were possible to administer the sleeping medication against her will. A re-examination of the victim took place. The idea was suggested by a fax from Mrs. De Ridder, Esquire (attachment 2) who doubted the state of mind necessary for a suicide, because her client made such a cheerful and positive impression. The correspondence of the last few months between Mrs. Vink, Mrs Sijtsma and Mrs. Staverman indicate the exact opposite to suicide.

Upon re-examination light bruises were found near the underside of the jaw. From this it was concluded that she must have been held down while her mouth was forced open. The drugged liquid was then administered. Unfortunately, because of the nature of the incident, this detail was overlooked during admission to the hospital. There seemed no point in looking for other causes.

The amount of sleeping pills was insufficient. Another mistake of the murderer. But because she is still in coma and there seem to be no signs of improvement, the perpetrator is still of the opinion that he has succeeded. He is still unaware of our evidence against suicide. And that is what will cost him his neck. To be on the safe side, I have posted a round-the-clock guard on Mrs. Staverman.

Certain that we would find out about his wife's earlier attempt at suicide, he counted on the fact that we would not further investigate a second attempt. He almost succeeded! Please refer to my fax of March 30. He carefully laid the groundwork by mentioning her earlier attempt and the subsequent psychiatric help to Mrs. Vink in Brunei.

Because of the correspondence between Mrs. Vink and Mrs. Sijtsma I was also confronted with the fire which destroyed part of their farm house in September of last year. As a result of the cooperation of the Maasland Fire Department (see attachment 3), we were able to compare the timing mechanisms found at the scene of the fire with the remnants of the detonating device found in the Toyota which ended the life of Hutters. Although the devices differ, the wiring in all devices is of the same material, most likely from the same roll (attachment 4).

Subject to further verification, this is the most likely scenario of past events: During the last days of their leave in August, Staverman installed an ignition in one of the timing devices used to switch lights on and off. He then made a small leak in the gas supply to the house. Enough gas collected in the house, after a time, to insure an explosion when a spark was generated by one of the timing devices. We don't know whether he caused the devices to spark regularly, so that the explosion would occur whenever enough gas was available, or whether he calculated that time and then set the device for that specific time.

Because of the straw roof, he could be reasonably sure that there would be precious little to find after the fire. Which proved to be the case. The question is, why the fire was needed at all. The answer is in the meticulous preparation of the entire operation. He found his accomplice, in the person of Hutters, during August. But he needed a means to dispose of Hutters from a distance whenever Hutters would find out too much, i.e. became dangerous. Why did he not make those arrangements in August, during his regular leave? Because everybody, colleagues in Brunei, Headquarters, friends, relatives, acquaintances, etc. knew that they would be in Holland during August. Upon further investigation this coincidence would most certainly be remarked upon and the possibility existed that the trail would lead to him. He also took into consideration that the lessor of the garage would possibly recognize him, later. Because of the fire, he was here for just one week, at his own expense. Private travel is not normally noted in the Shell leave records.

During that week he rented the garage. We showed his photograph to the owner of the garage, Mrs. School, and she declared under oath to recognize the man who had rented the garage from her, last October. Other matters were taken care of, during this week. He stole the Toyota on October 2 and, according to the sticker, installed the new battery on October 5. All of it, therefore during the period that he was here ostentatiously to take care of his house.

The Libyan mentioned in the fax from Brunei, must be the person who supplied the explosives. Perhaps he also arranged for the revolver, the bomb and detonation devices. Perhaps he also instructed Staverman in their use. Staverman was an ex-marine (see attachment 5), so could not have been totally unfamiliar with fire arms.

But how does one smuggle a revolver with silencer, explosives and detonation devices into Holland without using one of the illegal methods for doing so. With current airport security it is virtually impossible to get this type of material passed by the various check points, especially when travel originates in the Near East, or Far East. But a Shell employee, traveling on a Company Jet, can be allowed to transport a certain amount of household goods. It now becomes simple. This type of freight is seldom checked, according to my information.

Then the following: During what he calls "Phase 1",

while still in Brunei, our suspect needs information about Headquarters. That is to say, during the period that we received the faxes from the so-called Radical People's Front for Africa. He has to remain informed about the reaction within the firm. For this he created a beautiful connection: Hutters! But Hutters had left the firm. He knew that Hutters had become a bitter man, thus eminently usable. When he first contacted Hutters and made an agreement with him, he most certainly did not talk about killing the hostage. I am convinced, however, that he planned to kill Ron Voute from the very beginning. But Hutters saw a chance to get revenge and cooperated.

How did Hutters get his information? How was he able to get information almost directly from the Board Room? Because of the cleaning lady. Leni Kaluwe: two mornings a week at Mrs. Stork's (wife of Shell's Acting Managing Director) and two times a week at Mrs. Hutters. We interrogated Leni. She is a nice lady, but with a motor mouth. Everything she knows, learns, or hears is later, without any discrimination, repeated to whoever wants to listen. I called Mrs. Hutters and asked her how the relationship was between her husband and Leni. She told me that he liked Leni and sometimes would talk to her for an hour, or more, whenever Leni would take a "break". He also urged his wife to re-establish contact with Leonie Voute, supposedly to make an effort to rekindle old friendships.

When Hutters was liquidated, the information supplied by Leni dried up. But what does Mrs. Staverman write to Mrs Vink in Brunei? "I engaged her (Leni) on a permanent basis. Twice a week a half day. Not because I need the help, but Arie wanted that so . . ." The connection was re-established.

In addition, in the interest of completeness, we also checked again on the tennis court at The Hall. Because we were hampered by a need for secrecy during our initial investigations, we did not discover what we discovered during this later visit. The night that Mr. Voute played and won with 6-4, 6-3 there was a phone call around 11:30 PM. Somebody, who identified himself as a friend of Mr. Voute, asked for him. In passing, the caller asked the owner of the establishment the result of Mr. Voute's game.

Staverman has been almost continually one step ahead of us. First with the so-called "humane" goals of the organization. We wasted a lot of time on a wild goose chase for an organization that did not exist. He planned everything carefully. Every time he did something, he also made sure to place an obstacle in our path designed to make us draw the wrong conclusions. The fact that everything was accomplished by fax is extremely cunning and, if it was not because of the criminal intent, would almost force us to admire his methods. He knew that any personal contact, either by phone or by letter, would create unacceptable risks. This method also made him immune to any psychological pressures which could only be exerted during a dialogue. He was able to maintain a distance which, in similar kidnapping cases, has never been equalled.

I hereby request your presence in my office, after having read this fax. I would like you to be present when we arrest Arie Staverman and charge him with two counts of premeditated murder, attempted murder, extortion and kidnapping. Messrs. Stork and van de Brink have meanwhile been released.

The case is closed, but there is no reason to rejoice. Two people, one of which was completely innocent, have died. In retrospect it all seems so simple. After a case is solved you wonder how you could possibly have missed such obvious clues. We could have prevented all of this.

I can never completely get away from a certain feeling of guilt when a file is closed. Absolutely without reason, but it is difficult to feel otherwise. I never feel a sense of victory. That, in a way, is the tragedy of our profession. There are never any winners, just losers. The people who died unnecessarily and the people who are left behind to cope with the losses. I feel sorry for all of them. Mr. Voute, a brilliant career and a desirable social position resulted in the death of his only son. Mrs. Stork will have to face an uncertain future when her husband's financial speculations catch up with him. And Mrs. Staverman. Again alone in a world that has treated her less than fair already.

After too short a period of time, most everybody will have forgotten all about it. The person who only knows the case through the newspapers will forget and we, the police, will be deep into the next case. Everything goes on. Time heals all wounds, they say, but I wonder.

There are always those that remain ....

A.W. Vaart

TO MRS. CARLA VINK

Rotterdam, 4 April, 1990

Dear Carla:

Yvonne woke from her coma at 10:30 last night. She is doing well. I talked to her. As soon as she has recovered some more, she'll be allowed to talk to the police. I was there this morning and she told me how he forced her to drink the glass of water in which the sleeping pills had been dissolved.

I am going home now and will not be back. Frank promised to buy me a fax today, so you will be able to reach me at home. Don't expect any cheerful letters from me, for a while.

Janny

J.M. VOUTE, ESQUIRE
MRS. A.L. VOUTE-BERKHOVEN
CAMIN DU VILLE 29
VENCE 2898
FRANCE

Vence, June 10, 1990

Dear caring family and friends:

This letter is written by hand and will be mailed in the normal way, the way it used to be. No more faxes.

Time has passed, memories remain. We gratefully remember the days that we were able to bask in your support during the most difficult period of our life.

The loss we have suffered will forever remain on our minds and it will haunt us until the last days of our lives.

Everything has changed because of that. Nothing will ever be the same again. We have not answered any letters, nor have we responded to any other attempts at communication. This has gone on for months. We needed the time.

There would come a time, however, that we would again have the courage and the will to go outside ourselves. To meet again with people and to talk to them.

That day was a long time in coming. Longer than we expected. But everything is always different than expected. Especially when it comes to human wishes and desires.

But we have come out of our shell and we want you all to know that. We finally realized that we could not crawl away from everybody. We cannot forever nurse our grief.

We want to visit you all, soon. We want to meet you again and we want to make sure that the bonds that remain between us will not be lost again.

Leonie

Jan Vorster

About the Author:

Henk Elsink (ELSINCK) is a new star on the Dutch detective-thriller scene. His first book, "Tenerife!", received rave press reviews in the Netherlands. Among them: "A wonderful plot, well written." (De Volkskrant), "A successful first effort. A find!" (Het Parool) and "A jewel!" (Brabants Dagblad).

After a successful career as a stand-up comic and cabaretier, Elsinck retired as a star of radio, TV, stage and film and started to devote his time to the writing of books. He divides his time between Palma de Mallorca (Spain), Turkey and the Netherlands. He has written three books and a fourth is in progress.

Elsinck's books are as far-ranging as their author. His stories reach from Spain to Amsterdam, from Brunei to South America and from Italy to California. His books are genuine thrillers that will keep readers glued to the edge of their seats.

The author is a proven best-seller and the careful, authorized translations of his work, published by New Amsterdam Publishing should fascinate the English speaking world as it has the European reading public.

TENERIFE!

by Elsinck

Madrid 1989. The body of a man is found in a derelict hotel room. The body is suspended, by means of chains, from hooks in the ceiling. A gag protrudes from the mouth. He has been tortured to death. Even hardened police officers turn away, nauseated. And this won't be the only murder. Quickly the reader becomes aware of the identity of the perpetrator, but the police are faced with a complete mystery. What are the motives? It looks like revenge, but what do the victims have in common? Why does the perpetrator prefer black leather cuffs, blindfolds and whips? The hunt for the assassin leads the police to seldom frequented places in Spain and Amsterdam, including the little known world of the S&M clubs in Amsterdam's Red Light District. In this spine-tingling thriller the reader follows the hunters, as well as the hunted and Elsinck succeeds in creating near unendurable suspense.

First American edition of this European Best-Seller.

ISBN 1 881164 51 9

From critical reviews of **Tenerife!**:

... A wonderful plot, well written — Strong first effort — Promising debut — A successful first effort. A find! — A well written book, holds promise for the future of this author — A first effort to make dreams come true — A jewel of a thriller! — An excellent book, gripping, suspenseful and extremely well written ...

CONFESSION OF A HIRED KILLER

by Elsinck

A dead man is found in a small house on the remote Greek island of Serifos. His sole legacy consists of an incomplete letter, still in the typewriter. An intensive investigation reveals that the man may well be an independent, hired killer. His "clients" apparently included the Mafia and the Cosa Nostra. The trail leads from the Mediterranean to Berkeley, California and with quick scene changes and a riveting style, Elsinck succeeds again in creating a high tempo and sustained tension. A carefully documented thriller which exposes the merciless methods of organized crime. In 1990 Elsinck burst on the scene with the much talked-about *Tenerife!* which was followed, in 1991, with *Murder by Fax*. His latest offering has all the elements of another best-seller.

First American edition of this European Best-Seller.

ISBN 1 881164 53 5

From critical reviews of **Confession of a Hired Killer**:

... Elsinck remains a valuable asset to the thriller genre. He is original, writes in a lively style and researches his material with painstaking care ...

DeKok and Murder on the Menu
Baantjer

On the back of a menu from the Amsterdam Hotel-Restaurant *De Poort van Eden* (Eden's Gate) is found the complete, signed confession of a murder. The perpetrator confesses to the killing of a named blackmailer. Inspector DeKok (Amsterdam Municipal Police, Homicide) and his assistant, Vledder, gain possession of the menu. They remember the unsolved murder of a man whose corpse, with three bullet holes in the chest, was found floating in the waters of the Prince's Canal. A year-old case which was almost immediately turned over to the Narcotics Division. At the time it was considered to be just one more gang-related incident. DeKok and Vledder follow the trail of the menu and soon more victims are found and DeKok and Vledder are in deadly danger themselves. Although the murder was committed in Amsterdam, the case brings them to Rotterdam and other, well-known Dutch cities such as Edam and Maastricht.

First American edition of this European Best-Seller.

ISBN 1 881164 31 4

DeKok and the Somber Nude
Baantjer

The oldest of the four men turned to DeKok: "You're from Homicide?" DeKok nodded. The man wiped the raindrops from his face, bent down and carefully lifted a corner of the canvas. Slowly the head became visible: a severed girl's head. DeKok felt the blood drain from his face. "Is that all you found?" he asked. "A little further," the man answered sadly, "is the rest." Spread out among the dirt and the refuse were the remaining parts of the body: both arms, the long, slender legs, the petite torso. There was no clothing.

First American edition of this European Best-Seller.

ISBN 1 881164 01 2

Baantjer's laconic, rapid-fire story telling has spun out a surprisingly complex web of mysteries.
                                                    —Kirkus Reviews

DeKok and the Dead Harlequin
Baantjer

Murder, double murder, is committed in a well-known Amsterdam hotel. During a nightly conversation with the murderer DeKok tries everything possible to prevent the murderer from giving himself up to the police. Risking the anger of superiors DeKok disappears in order to prevent the perpetrator from being found. But he is found, thanks to a six-year old girl who causes untold misery for her family by refusing to sleep. A respected citizen, head of an important Accounting Office is deadly serious when he asks for information from the police. He is planning to commit murder. He decides that DeKok, as an expert, is the best possible source to teach him how to commit the perfect crime.

First American edition of this European Best-Seller.

ISBN 1 881164 04 7

DeKok and the Sorrowing Tomcat
Baantjer

Peter Geffel (Cunning Pete) had to come to a bad end. Even his Mother thought so. Still young, he dies a violent death. Somewhere in the sand dunes that help protect the low lands of the Netherlands he is found by an early jogger, a dagger protruding from his back. The local police cannot find a clue. They inform other jurisdictions via the police telex. In the normal course of events, DeKok (Homicide) receives a copy of the notification. It is the start of a new adventure for DeKok and his inseparable side-kick, Vledder. Baantjer relates the events in his usual, laconic manner.

First American edition of this European Best-Seller.

ISBN 1 881164 05 5

DeKok and the Disillusioned Corpse
Baantjer

DeKok watched, flanked by his assistant Vledder, as two men from the coroner's office fished a corpse from the waters of the Brewer's Canal. The deceased was a young men with a sympathetic face. Vledder looked and then remarked: "I don't know, but I have the feeling that this one could cause us a lot of trouble. I don't like that strange wound on his head. He also doesn't seem the type to just walk into the water." Vledder was right. Leon, aka Jacques, or Marcel, was the victim of a crime. The solution poses a lot of riddles.

First American edition of this European Best-Seller.

ISBN 1 881164 06 3

DeKok and the Careful Killer
Baantjer

The corpse of a young woman is found in the narrow, barely lit alley in one of the more disreputable areas of Amsterdam. She is dressed in a chinchilla coat, an expensive, leather purse is found near her right shoulder and it looks as if she died of cramps. The body is twisted and distorted. Again DeKok and his invaluable assistant, Vledder, are involved in a new mystery. There are no clues, no motives and, apparently, no perpetrators. But the young woman has been murdered. *That* is certain. Eventually, of course, DeKok unmasks the careful murderer, but not before the reader has taken a trip through the seamier parts of Amsterdam.

First American edition of this European Best-Seller.

ISBN 1 881164 07 1

Murder in Amsterdam
Baantjer

The two very first "DeKok" stories for the first time in a single volume. In these stories DeKok meets Vledder, his invaluable assistant, for the first time. The book contains two complete novels. In *DeKok and the Sunday Strangler*, DeKok is recalled from his vacation in the provinces and tasked to find the murderer of a prostitute. The young, "scientific" detectives are stumped. A second murder occurs, again on Sunday and under the same circumstances. No sign of a struggle, or any other kind of resistance. Because of a circumstantial meeting, with a "missionary" to the Red Light District, DeKok discovers how the murderer thinks. At the last moment DeKok is able to prevent a third murder. In *DeKok and the Corpse on Christmas Eve*, a patrolling constable notices a corpse floating in the Gentlemen's Canal. Autopsy reveals that she has been strangled and that she was pregnant. "Silent witnesses" from the purse of the murdered girl point to two men who played an important role in her life. The fiancee could not possibly have committed the murder, but who is the second man? In order to preserve his Christmas Holiday, DeKok wants to solve the case quickly.

First American edition of these European Best-Sellers in a single volume.

ISBN 1 881164 00 4

Both stories are very easy to take. —**Kirkus Reviews**

About Baantjer:

Albert Cornelis Baantjer (BAANTJER) is the most widely read author in the Netherlands. In a country with less than 15 million inhabitants he sold, in 1988, his millionth "DeKok" book. Todate more than 35 titles in his "DeKok" series have been written and more than 2.5 million copies have been sold. Baantjer can safely be considered a publishing phenomenon. In addition he has written other fiction and non-fiction and writes a daily column for a Dutch newspaper. It is for his "DeKok" books, however, that he is best known. *Every* year more than 70,000 Dutch people check a "Baantjer/DeKok" out of a library. The Dutch version of the Reader's Digest Condensed Books (called "Best Books" in Holland) has selected a Baantjer/DeKok book five (5) times for inclusion in its series of condensed books.

Baantjer writes about Detective-Inspector DeKok of the Amsterdam Municipal Police (Homicide). Baantjer is himself an ex-inspector of the Amsterdam Police and is able to give his fictional characters the depth and the personality of real characters encountered during his long police career. Many people in Holland sometimes confuse real-life Baantjer with fictional DeKok. The author has never before been translated.

This author is a proven best-seller and the careful, authorized translations of his work, published by New Amsterdam Publishing should fascinate the English speaking world as it has the Dutch reading public.